Whiskey Tango Foxtrot

Tales of the Forgotten

By W. J. Lundy

Whiskey Tango Foxtrot
© 2013 W. J. Lundy

Escaping the Dead
Tales of the Forgotten

This book is a work of fiction. The names, characters, places and incidents are products of the writer's imagination or have been used fictitiously and are not to be construed as real. Any resemblance to persons, living or dead, actual events, locales or organizations is entirely coincidental. All Rights Are Reserved. No part of this book may be used or reproduced in any manner whatsoever without written permission from the author.

Whiskey Tango Foxtrot
Escaping the Dead
By W. J. Lundy

Note from the Author:

I wrote the short story Whiskey Tango Foxtrot while serving overseas in Afghanistan; it was roughly fifty pages longhand when I first put it together. I initially released as a digital short novella, it did very well, and gathered enough interest that I was motivated to finish the full length novel.

Because the short story is only fifty pages, I didn't think it would be feasible to have it printed and published. But I didn't want it to just go away or only be available to a kindle audience, so… I snuck it into the Novel. At the end of the short story you will find the Tales of the Forgotten. I hope you enjoy it, and thank you for reading.

WJ Lundy

Whiskey Tango Foxtrot

Escaping the Dead

© 2013 W. J. Lundy

This book is a work of fiction. The names, characters, places and incidents are products of the writer's imagination or have been used fictitiously and are not to be construed as real. Any resemblance to persons, living or dead, actual events, locales or organizations is entirely coincidental. All Rights Are Reserved. No part of this book may be used or reproduced in any manner whatsoever without written permission from the author.

The gravel crunched under the heavy wheels of the Mine Resistant Ambush Protected Vehicle (MRAP). Staff Sergeant Brad Thompson looked out of his passenger window, tirelessly searching and scanning for threats. A short, four-hour patrol to recon a village was how they'd been briefed, but they had already been on the trail for over five. First, a suspected roadside bomb had slowed their approach to the village, and then their radios had failed shortly after arriving. To make matters worse, confusion and lack of communications had caused an argument that further delayed their return to Forward Operating Base Bremmel.

Nobody wanted to be alone on the roads after dark, especially in an area where the Taliban owned the night. Brad's men were hungry and tired but still remained vigilant. His driver, Henry, was gripping the wheel tight, and Brad reminded him to stay focused. Cole the gunner was on the .50 caliber machine gun up in the turret. Brad could hear the squeaking of gears when Cole rotated the turret to get a better angle on blind spots as they drove down the dusty trail.

Suddenly the vehicles ahead all began to slow, then came to a stop. Brad's headset squelched and he heard Lieutenant Rogers call his leaders forward to the command vehicle. Brad undid his harness while telling Cole to keep scanning his sector for targets. "Henry ... I'm going forward to see the lieutenant," Brad said in a tired voice. He opened the door and took the long step down, bracing himself for the drop. Gripping his M4 with his dominant hand, he swung down. Landing hard, he began the walk forward.

Passing the dusty vehicles, he looked inside and saw the tired and drawn faces of the passengers. He found the lieutenant leaning over the hood of an older, armored-style Humvee. Lieutenant Rogers was talking to their platoon sergeant, Sergeant First Class Turner, and a couple of the other squad leaders about the return trip to Bremmel. They all had disgusted looks on their faces, and Brad worried the argument from earlier would kick back in.

"Staff Sergeant Thompson, glad you could join us," complained SFC Turner. "I was just trying to explain to the lieutenant that this communication outage makes no sense. All of our internal radios are working, and we should have been able to pick up the FOB once we cleared that last ridge. We still aren't picking up shit. We ain't even seen any aircraft in the last three hours."

Brad scratched at the five o'clock shadow on his chin. Turner was right, it didn't make sense. He had never experienced anything like this. Even though the butt of many jokes, military radios had almost always been reliable. "What about the Blue Force Tracker?" Brad asked.

"It's still not working, I mean, we can navigate but nobody is sending messages or replying to mine," the lieutenant answered. "This isn't right! It's all wrong," he mumbled. "I want suggestions, and I want them now. I don't want to continue down this road with no comms and no air support."

Brad paused apprehensively before he began to speak. "Let's halt here, Lieutenant. We can hold back the main body and set up a defensive perimeter.

I can take my gun truck and two of the lighter Humvees back up the road to Bremmel. Without the main body we can move faster and avoid threats. When I reach Bremmel, we can figure out what's up with the comms and send a couple birds back to escort the rest of you home."

Turner shook his head and grimaced. "I don't like the idea of splitting our force when I don't know what's lurking out there ... But it may be the best course for what we got going."

"Okay then, let's stop wasting time. Sergeant Thompson, pull your truck ahead and get ready to move out with two trucks from second squad. I want you guys rolling in five mikes," Lieutenant Rogers barked.

Brad walked back to his truck and jumped into the passenger seat. "Alright fellas, let's mount up. We're going to break out of the formation and move to the front."

"What's up Sergeant? What's going on?" asked Cole.

"We are going to route recon ahead and link back up with Raider at Bremmel. If we move fast, we can make it back in time for dinner," answered Brad.

"Hell, yeah! I hear that, Sarge," answered Henry as he pulled the MRAP out of the column and slowly moved to the front of the convoy.

As the MRAP passed the front vehicle, two more trucks dropped in behind them and they picked up speed. Brad lifted the radio handset and announced, "Charlie six, Charlie four, radio check."

"Charlie Four, this is Six, I read you loud and clear," came the response.

"Roger that Six, Charlie Four on mission," Brad answered. "Hey Henry, how 'bout you put that pedal down and get us home. Cole, keep your eyes open and on the horizon. I don't want any surprises."

The MRAP roared as it picked up speed, and they quickly moved east along the road, throwing dust behind them.

Things really were strange. The road to FOB Bremmel was typically quiet in the daytime, especially by late afternoon, but they were used to at least seeing a shepherd or a stray jingle truck. Today they hadn't seen anything moving west away from the base. Brad started to get a bad feeling and consciously noticed his heart rate begin to quicken. They were now less than five miles from the base.

Brad keyed the mic on his radio handset and tried to call FOB Bremmel. "Task Force Raider, this is Charlie Four over." Brad heard nothing but static and tried again. "Task Force Raider, this is Charlie Four over." Again nothing. He tried the convoy. "Charlie Six, this is Charlie Four over."

"Go for Six," squelched back on the radio.

"This is Charlie Four, still no response from Raider."

"Roger understood, stay on mission, Six out," came the answer from the radio.

Brad looked to the left and could see the worry on Henry's face. Things definitely were not right. Brad checked in with the two scout vehicles behind him and asked them to tighten up the formation as they got closer to Bremmel. They moved down into a saddle and up the other side as they made their final approach towards the road to the FOB's front gate. They reached the top and made a hard turn onto the paved road. Henry slammed on the brakes and everything in the truck crashed forward. Brad heard the trucks behind skidding to a stop. "What the fuck, Henry!" Brad shouted, and then looked up and saw FOB Bremmel.

The FOB was burning. There were people running all along the perimeter, pouring over the walls. There was no gunfire, but the base was being mobbed.

"Permission to open fire!" Cole shouted.

"No! Hold your fire. They are out of range anyhow and we don't know what's happening," Brad shouted back.

Panicked, Henry looked to Brad. "Jesus! Sergeant, what's going on down there? Why is there no gunfire? Did we lose the base? What's going on?"

"Everyone lock it down. Cole, keep your eyes on that gun." There was a knock on his side window. It was Corporal Méndez from the Humvee that had been behind them.

"This is bad, Sarge, what is this? How could all of them civilians take out the base? What are we going to do?" he asked.

"Méndez, get back to your truck. Get your guns up and keep an eye out. It looks like nobody has noticed us up here. I want to keep it that way. I'll be with you in a minute," Brad answered as he lifted his radio handset. "Charlie Six, this is Four."

"Go for Six."

"Six, this is Four, we are one click from Bremmel. Bremmel is overrun."

"Repeat your last, Charlie Four."

"I said we are one click from Bremmel … Break … The base has been overrun and is burning!" he yelled into the handset.

"Calm down, Sergeant, I need you to give me a clear answer on what you are seeing."

"I told you! The base is overrun with civilians … the gate is open and it's burning."

"Wait one Sergeant, we have a group of civilians approaching the back of our perimeter," came the reply from the radio.

Cole spoke from up in the turret. "Sergeant, you might want to look at this."

Brad turned his attention from the radio and looked up. He saw that a small ant trail of people were moving out of the base and headed in their direction. They were moving fast, not quite a run, but definitely at a quick pace.

"Charlie Six, we are being approached by the mob from the base, please advise," he said into the radio.

"Charlie Four break contact, return to the convoy" **crack crack crack** *"we are under assault, we are engaging with less than lethal. Return to the convoy."*

"Roger, Charlie Six, we are enroute."

"Less than lethal not working, they are swamping the—" **crack crack crack** *"trucks ... they are dragging off the crews! ... Open fire!"*

"Charlie Six, this is Four. What's going on?" Brad yelled into the handset.

"Uhhh, Sergeant! They are getting closer!" yelled Cole, now in a panic.

Brad looked up and saw the approaching mob was now inside of a thousand meters and moving very quickly. He lifted his M4 to use the advanced optics to get a better look. He could see a large group had now separated itself from the main ant trail, and was distancing itself from the rest of the group. He looked at the man in front. He was wearing a traditional men's dress but his head was bare and so were his feet. The man was at a fast jog, his face was filled with rage, and those behind him looked the same. Then Brad noticed with alarm that the man's chest was covered in blood. He scanned the crowd; they also were covered in dark stains.

"Cole, give them a burst ... Keep it far off! I don't want you hitting them by accident," Brad ordered.

"On the way," Cole responded.

The large weapon thumped in a quick report as it poured a six-round burst out towards the approaching mob. Rounds skipped off the ground in front of them, kicking up sparks and dust. They didn't even flinch; they kept running at the same pace without missing a beat.

Henry was becoming panicked; he was shaking in his seat. "This isn't good Sarge, we should leave."

Brad didn't look away to answer; he was fixed on the mob. They were seconds' away and building speed, and then they hit the vehicles like a tidal wave. The armored MRAP shuddered but took the impact.

"Cole! Button up!" Brad screamed.

Cole dropped into the vehicle, slamming and locking the hatch shut behind him. Bodies tried to climb up the truck, having trouble because of the vehicle's towering height, but the two Humvees didn't have the same luck.

Brad heard the gun from Méndez's truck fire, and looked back; he could see the mob swarming over the vehicle. In the turret, Méndez's gunner was being grabbed at. He was firing madly, and the Humvee took off, wildly out of control. The third truck was backing up, trying to escape the mob. Brad saw the empty turret but couldn't see if the gunner had been able to escape and close his hatch. The Humvee was being pressed against the stone wall behind it. Suddenly, he saw the gunner hadn't escaped; he was being ripped apart by the mob. He could see a bloody flurry of activity in the cab of the Humvee.

"Henry! Drive! Get us out of here," Brad yelled.

Henry hit the accelerator hard. The huge MRAP lurched forward, making a sickening crunch as it plowed over and through the mob. They were still climbing and holding on to the sides of the vehicle. Henry was pulling away from the crowd. Méndez's vehicle was moving alongside. He could see that Méndez's truck had finally closed its hatch, but still had about eight of the crazies holding onto the top.

"Cole, can you see Truck Three?" Brad yelled.

"It's lost, Sergeant, the doors are open and those guys are dragging them out. What the fuck? They are ripping them apart!" he shouted back.

"Get it together guys! Henry, calm down and drive right. Those fucks aren't getting in this truck. We will deal with them when we get away from that mob."

They drove for what seemed like an eternity. The crazies were still banging and pounding on the sides of the armored vehicle. Every now and then one would tumble onto the hood of the truck or fall off the side. No one said anything. The men just stayed focused, Henry hunched over the wheel. Finally the internal radio broke the silence and Brad's headset squelched.

"Sergeant? What just happened?" It was Méndez from the trail vehicle.

"I don't know. We need to get back to the convoy," Brad answered.

"Sergeant, we can't see Jones and Truck Three; we have to go back."

"Truck Three is gone. There is no going back there. What's your crew's status, Corporal?"

"We're okay but my gunner is fucked up, and those guys are still on the roof. Looks like you have a bunch on you also."

"Okay Corporal, take care of your gunner. Follow us, I'll be back with you in a minute." Brad reached for his radio handset and tried to call the convoy; after three tries and no response, he gave up.

"Méndez, I think we are alone here. We have to lose these shitheads on our vehicles. Do you understand?" Brad said into his internal mic.

"I understand Sarge. What do you want me to do?"

"We're going to stop. You stop about twenty feet away and I'm going to shoot the bastards off of your truck," Brad answered.

Brad asked Henry to slow the vehicle and turn it so his firing portal faced Méndez's truck. When the vehicle had come to a complete stop, the things on top got frenzied. Brad could hear them clawing and pounding at the armor above. Brad knew in that moment that the enemy outside wasn't human. They didn't behave rationally. He didn't know what they were, but they weren't people. Not anymore.

He eased open his firing port just enough so that he could fit the barrel of his M4 out. He had a small internal debate in his head: whether or not it was okay to shoot one of these unarmed civilians, human or not. But then the answer came back to him, in the vision of Truck Three's gunner being torn apart. He looked through his optics and took aim at one of the crazies on Méndez's truck. He put the cross hair center mass on a large male that had his fingers wedged into the door jam. He pulled the trigger and felt the recoil in his shoulder. *'Nothing! Damn. I missed?'* He took aim and fired again; this time the man's left arm went limp but he still howled and pried at the door with his right. Brad looked through the sight and fired four more times. Finally the man loosened his grip and fell to a knee, then tumbled off the truck.

"Holy shit! How in the hell did that just happen? That freak just took six shots. This shit ain't right, Sarge," Cole shouted as he watched through his own portal.

Brad ignored him, taking aim on the next one, an overweight man sitting on the hood. This time he aimed at the head, and blew the man's brains out onto the windshield. He finished off one more the same way.

"Now it's your turn, Méndez," he said into his headset.

"Roger. I'm on it," came the reply.

He watched as Méndez slowly opened his armored window and fired off close to thirty rounds before he announced that the MRAP was clear. They sat quietly for a minute before Brad decided to get out.

Brad undid the combat lock and slowly opened the door. He looked over and saw that Méndez was also exiting his vehicle. Brad stepped to the ground and saw one of the bodies lying in a slump near a tire. The man looked like he had been clawed and bitten; maybe as a result of the rough ride on the MRAP? He saw a leg hanging from the top of the truck. He grabbed for it and pulled the body free of the vehicle. It hit the ground with a thud. It was a female wearing a light shirt. Brad could see she had taken several shots from Méndez's rifle and her wounds were covered in fresh blood. She also had several deep cuts and at least one older bullet wound in her abdomen.

"What is this?" Méndez said. Brad turned and saw Méndez standing behind him.

"I don't know, man, but I know we killed them. Maybe it's a bio weapon, you know terrorist are always into some crazy shit."

"You heard from the convoy?" asked Méndez.

"No man, I'm kind of hoping the radio is out. My antenna looks like it was ripped off. Last I heard they were engaging a mob. I hope it's not the same shit we just saw. How is your gunner?"

"He is bad, Sergeant. Those things tried to pull him out of the hatch. He had his harness on, but they still dislocated his shoulder. Looks like one of them took a bite out of his forearm."

Brad walked over to Méndez's truck. They had Private First Class Ryan laid out in the back. Ryan had sweat dripping off of him and a tourniquet on his arm. Méndez's medic and driver, Specialist Eric, was treating him.

Eric looked up as he saw Brad. "I don't get it, Sarge. He's burning up with fever. He hasn't woken up since he passed out after the attack. I started an IV, but I don't think it's helping."

"Okay … Good job soldier, just do the best you can. We're going to mount up and try to get back to the convoy. We'll get him help soon."

Beep Beep Beep. Brad turned his attention to his MRAP. Henry was beating the horn. He leaned his head out of the window and frantically yelled, "Sergeant, they're back about five thousand meters and on the run."

"Cole! Get that gun up, suppress and take them out!" Brad yelled.

"On the way, Sergeant," Cole answered as he racked the M2 machine gun, chambering a round, then pointed it in the direction of the closing mob.

"Méndez, mount up and get ready to move," Brad ordered.

Thump, thump, thump, thump. Cole had started firing his big gun. Brad climbed into his seat and secured his door. He watched Méndez's truck pull around and angle behind him.

"Let's go! Back to the convoy, Henry. Cole, keep pouring it on them!" shouted Brad.

He looked back through the window and could see the mob cresting the hill, now just meters from where they had been. Cole was knocking them down with the big gun; he paused only to reload. Brad saw some of them moving on the ground and then get back up. *'What the hell?'* he thought. *'Nobody takes a fifty caliber round and survives.'* He looked through his scope and saw a man limping down the road with a softball-size holed near his hip, but he was still trying to jog after them. After about five yards, the man fell flat on his face. Eventually the pack faded from view and Brad ordered Cole to cease fire.

Henry spoke first. "Sergeant, how is that possible? We are almost ten miles from the FOB and those things caught up with us. They aren't Kenyans, Sarge! Nobody is that fast, they didn't even look tired."

"I don't know, Henry. I shot that guy six times before he went down. Cole was tearing that crowd apart with the big gun, and I swear I saw some of them get back up. Let's just keep it together and we'll figure this out."

Brad spoke into the internal radio. "Méndez, take point and recon ahead. I don't want any surprises up front."

The more maneuverable Humvee passed the MRAP and pulled away. Méndez's truck was far ahead now and running as a scout, staying just within sight of Brad.

They drove for close to an hour without seeing anything or hearing a word on the radio. It was getting late and the sun was beginning to crest the mountains. Brad knew they would only have another hour or so of daylight.

"Sergeant, I can see the convoy. I'm stopping," squelched the radio.

"Roger that, Méndez, we'll hang back. What can you see?" asked Brad.

"Not good, Sarge, I can see the vehicles, looks like maybe one or two are missing. There are no people. Nothing appears to be alive down there."

"Stay in position Méndez. I'm moving to your location," Brad responded.

The MRAP moved forward and pulled up alongside the Humvee. Brad used his scout binos to look at the scene ahead of him.

"Looks like the lieutenant circled the wagons," he muttered. The convoy was still in its defensive perimeter. Brad didn't see anyone in the turrets, and the razor wire barrier looked like it had been dragged inside their safe zone.

Brad continued to scan but he didn't see a single living person. Most of the vehicles had their doors open, and the turrets still had mounted weapons on top. Brad knew his people wouldn't leave their vehicles and weapons like that. He did a vehicle count and compared it with the convoy order he had received early that morning. Two MRAPS were missing from the convoy.

Brad had an idea of what might have happened by the way things were strewn about. The perimeter had been overrun and the lighter vehicles had easily been overtaken in the same way they had lost Truck Three. The heavier MRAPs were able to take the initial blow and remain secured. Brad guessed that the MRAPs had fled the mob and were pursued by the attackers in the same way the Bremmel mob had chased his team.

With his two vehicles on line, they approached the perimeter. As they got closer, he could tell that it wasn't going to be pretty. The soldiers hadn't abandoned their positions. Parts of them were scattered everywhere, as well as several bodies of the crazies that had attacked the convoy. They pulled to within one hundred meters of the perimeter. He had Cole and Eric mount the guns and provide cover while he and Méndez went in on foot. Not only did he want to protect his men from any physical danger, he wanted to save them from the experience of finding their friends slaughtered.

As he walked through the wreckage, it was clear the soldiers had put up a fight. There was blood everywhere; pieces of body armor and protective equipment had been torn apart and were strewn around. Brad saw a fighting position with a pile of brass and dead bodies. Many of the dead were slashed and cut apart. Located near the pile was a dead soldier Brad recognized, still with a fighting knife in his hand.

They found the lieutenant's Humvee with the doors open and bent. The inside of the truck was smeared with blood, and its contents were tossed everywhere. One MRAP had dead bodies draped all over it and surrounding it, all shredded by the MRAP's fifty caliber machine gun.

'Whoever manned that gun must have gone down hard,' Brad thought.

"Over here!" Méndez called.

Off to the side of the perimeter, they could see where sets of big tire tracks led away from the fight; it appeared that the vehicles had dragged the defensive razor wire with them. There was a trail of bodies marking where the vehicle tracks veered away into the distance. From the tracks and drag marks, it was obvious that the mob had followed them into the desert.

They found nothing else. They took a trailer off one of the MRAPs and loaded it with anything they could find in the convoy that they might need later: cases of MREs, bottled water, five-gallon cans of fuel, batteries, and as many ammo cans as they could carry. They grabbed a spare gun for each truck and called for Henry to bring down their vehicles so they could connect the trailer and top them off with fuel. Méndez located a sniper rifle and a couple of light 240B machine guns that he loaded in the rear of the MRAP.

After they were sure everything useful had been recovered, they mounted back up. Brad decided it was best to stay the night near the convoy in hopes the two MRAPs would circle back. He directed the vehicles off road and towards a small ridgeline that overlooked the convoy's final resting place. They pulled into a nice hide where the vehicles could be hidden by some large rock formations, but were still able to see the road and the approach to the ambush site.

The men were exhausted. Brad told them he would take the first watch, and instructed the others to get some rest. He walked over to check on PFC Ryan. He was still hot with fever and unconscious. The wounds around his forearm had grown a deep purple and there were angry streaks going up his arm. It didn't look good. He was still laid out in the back of the Humvee. Quietly, Brad closed the door and walked past Eric and Méndez who were sleeping off to the front of his truck.

He climbed on top of his MRAP and slowly scanned the horizon with his night vision scope, looking for any danger. Finding none, he settled into a comfortable position and carefully watched the road. The desert had become quiet and lonely in the twilight hours, the shadows growing as the sun slowly dropped behind the distant mountains.

Later, in the darkness, he heard moans and crowd noise coming from the road. Through his scope he could see the mob from Bremmel moving towards the convoy ambush site. The group paused when they reached the vehicles. Brad felt the hairs stand on the back of his neck while he waited to see what they would do. He looked behind him and could see that the rest of his men were also up and looking at the road.

The mob suddenly started moving again and continued to follow the road which led to the village that Brad and his men had patrolled earlier that day. Brad was relieved that the crazies didn't appear to be good trackers. Once again it became quiet, which was strange for this part of Afghanistan, where you could always hear jet aircraft or distant explosions all through the night.

Brad watched for an hour more, and then woke Henry to take over. He climbed into the back of the MRAP and drifted off to sleep, listening to Henry shuffle around on top of the large vehicle.

He woke to the muffled sounds of screaming. It wasn't his men; it was a loud howling moan, almost inhuman. He jumped out of his MRAP and saw his men gathered around the Humvee.

They were stone silent in disbelief. Inside, PFC Ryan was clawing at the doors and tugging on the handles trying to get out. Ryan's face was a mask of rage.

"I don't know what happened, Sergeant! I heard a noise in the Humvee and when I got close Ryan saw me and just started screaming. He's going crazy in there. I don't dare open the door," Cole said.

"It's okay, Cole, you were right not to open it or let him out. I'm not sure what's going on, but looks like he may be infected with whatever turned those people on the road," Brad answered.

"What do we do with him?" asked Cole.

Eric stepped between the men and the Humvee. "We can't kill him like the others. He's one of us."

Cole raised his hand and pointed at the vehicle, "He's making too much noise. He'll attract the crazies. We have to shut him up!"

"What the fuck do you mean 'shut him up'?" countered Eric.

"I mean if he doesn't stop screaming he is going to get us all killed," Cole shouted back.

Brad just looked on. "He's right," he said, raising his hand, "and we've got to silence him."

Eric stood his ground in front of them and pleaded, "Okay, you guys open the door. I'll tackle him and we can zip tie him and cover his mouth … We don't know what this is. Maybe it will wear off. Maybe there's a cure."

"Fine, let's do it then. Let's get this done quickly," replied Brad.

The men gathered around the Humvee door on the far side. The plan was for Cole to open the door, and when Ryan ran out at Brad and Méndez, Henry and Cole would drop a canvas tarp over him and wrestle him to the ground. Meanwhile Eric would apply the restraints to his wrists, then gag him.

As soon as they opened the door, Brad knew their plan wasn't going to work. He could see by the fear in the other men's eyes that they knew it also. Ryan wasn't a big man, and he wasn't considered strong, but this version of Ryan did not tire out. Ryan kept fighting and clawing at the canvas. He bit at Brad's leg through the tarp and the pain was unreal. Lucky for Brad, Ryan's teeth couldn't get through the heavy material.

They struggled with Ryan until they were all near exhaustion. Eric had only managed to put one wrist in a zip cuff, and it was taking everything Méndez and Brad had to keep Ryan's head pinned to the ground. The whole time Ryan was letting out screams of rage. Brad's arms began to get numb and he lost his grip. Even with the bad shoulder and bandaged arm, Ryan gained leverage. He was able to get a foot planted and he began to stand. Easily, he tossed Henry from his back, grabbed at Eric's pants, and then started to lunge. Suddenly, his body went limp and he slumped to the ground on top of Eric, his single zip tied hand gripping Eric's throat. There was a knife planted square in the back of Ryan's head.

"I'm sorry, it was too much, I didn't have a choice," cried Méndez.

"Wha ... wha ... You murdered him! You killed Ryan," Eric squealed.

With no thought, Brad slapped Eric and yelled, "Shut the fuck up, that wasn't Ryan! He would have killed all of us. I don't know what's happening but if we're going to make it … you better harden the fuck up!"

Brad paused for a moment before he continued. "Méndez! Grab your shovel and help me bury this soldier. The rest of you get packed up. We are rolling out of here as soon as it gets light."

Méndez and Brad lifted Ryan's limp body and carried him away from the trucks. They took one of his dog tags and his wallet. They put his military ID card and another tag in Ryan's breast pocket and buried him in the sand. They didn't say a word. When they were finished they quietly walked back to their vehicles.

Brad went straight to the MRAP and saw Cole helping Eric load his gear into the back of the truck. "What's going on, Cole?" Brad said.

"Well, Eric doesn't want to ride in that Humvee after what happened, and I tend to agree with him. Besides, this way we can ride together and we can save on fuel. Who knows how far we will have to drive?" Cole answered. Brad nodded his agreement and helped them cross-load the rest of their gear from the Humvee.

They pulled out of the hide at first light. Not really knowing where to go, they decided the best bet was to follow the two MRAPs that had fled the mob ambush on the road. Their MRAP now had two more passengers, bringing the crew to five. It was a bit more crowded, but they did feel more secure being locked tight in one vehicle, and Méndez and Eric were glad to be out of the Humvee after what had happened there. They drove past the quiet ambush site of the convoy, and fell into the tire tracks of the two missing vehicles.

After a good hour of driving they saw a makeshift campsite surrounded by a pile of bodies. "They must have discovered what we did yesterday, the bastards like to follow," said Brad.

"From the looks of it the guards spotted them early, and took off before they got close. We're still a good hundred feet from the stop site," said Cole.

Méndez stood to look out of the turret. "Good for them, maybe we'll have some good news today."

They settled back into the MRAP and continued to follow the trail. They drove all day and never saw anything else. When it got dark they decided to continue on, in hopes of meeting up with the missing vehicles. Brad eventually dozed off, lulled by the motion of the vehicle.

Henry woke Brad up with a shake. "Sergeant, where now?" It was early morning and the moon was still bright in the sky. They had come to a paved road, and the tracks ended. It was hard to tell which way the trucks had gone. Brad exited his MRAP and took a knee on the pavement, searching for clues. He could see where the mob of crazies had entered the road, but it didn't look like they knew which direction to go either. Some of the pack appeared to have just crossed the road and kept going. The rest traveled both left and right as if they couldn't make a decision. Brad was surprised that they didn't stick together; maybe they didn't have the pack mentality he'd expected.

He stood and walked back towards the truck, stopping when he heard a distant, familiar buzzing. He looked up and saw a small predator drone circling high above. Brad waved at the drone and turned on his IR strobe, hoping to let the drone know that he saw it. The drone reversed the direction of its orbit and reversed it again. Brad took this as a sign they had been seen, but he still didn't know what to do. Then the drone went to a lower altitude and followed the road to the north before going higher and back out of sight.

Brad entered the vehicle and said, "Well I guess that settles that, follow the drone."

"But Sergeant, that's away from the main base. Nothing is that way but Uzbekistan," argued Méndez.

"Corporal, it's almost four hundred kilometers to the main air base; we aren't going to make it there on our fuel and in these conditions. The border crossing at Hairatan is our best bet. There's a railroad and a lot of truck traffic there so somebody should see us. The drone saw us, so they know where we're at. Hopefully we can join up with the other trucks and they will send someone for us." The men reluctantly nodded in agreement, and Henry pulled the truck onto the road and headed north.

The going was slow. The MRAP rolled along at close to forty miles an hour on the blacktop. It wasn't a well-maintained road, and they had to stay aware of obstacles and potholes; this was no time for a broken axle. Brad had traveled the Hairatan road early in his tour and knew that it ended at a bridge and border crossing. Last time he was there, he'd visited the small Afghan Army post and had lunch with some of the U.S. soldiers who were stationed there as trainers and advisors. He hoped they were still there.

Henry stopped the truck again. Brad looked up and saw a silent MRAP sitting in the center of the road. Nothing moved around the lonely vehicle. The sun had just come up, and they could see that the doors were all closed.

"Bring it in slow, Henry," Brad said.

Henry eased the truck forward and when they were about fifty feet away Brad told him to stop. Cole was already in the turret and said he saw no movement. Brad, Méndez, and Eric dismounted the MRAP and slowly approached the vehicle.

"Cover me while I move up," Brad ordered the two soldiers behind him.

He slowly crept forward and hugged the back corner of the large vehicle. He looked for signs of people but found nothing. He put a foot on the back step and raised himself up to peek into the truck. It appeared empty, and unlike the vehicles at the ambush site, this one had the gun removed from the turret. Brad walked around to the driver's door and slowly opened it while trying to keep his M4 aimed with his free hand. The door squeaked open to reveal an empty cab. Brad stepped up into the vehicle to find a handwritten note.

Anyone who finds this.

We are the six survivors of Echo Company, 2nd Brigade. We were attacked on route A62 by a large population that approached us yesterday in the late afternoon. They ignored warnings from our roadblock to stop, and kept running for our perimeter. We used the limited bean bag shotgun rounds to try and turn them, but they had no effect. We opened up with our rifles, but we were quickly overrun, and they were in so close it was hard to fire effectively without hitting each other.

Most of our men were on the perimeter and were not able to flee to the safety of armored vehicles; several of us were able to board two MRAPS, but because of the mass of people we could provide little to no covering fire, instead we fled like cowards. As we left we could see our brothers fighting hand to hand, but they had little chance when up against 100 to 1 odds. We pushed our way out of the perimeter and into the desert with at least twenty of the things holding onto our trucks. We took turns shooting at each other's vehicles through the firing ports until we lost the clingers.

We drove for several hours before stopping and resting for the night. Within a couple hours our guards heard the mob approaching, but this time we were ready and we opened up with our 50 cal and the light machine gun on the other truck. The Mob went down but they didn't stop, soon they closed to within one hundred meters and we were forced again to run.

It appears that this enemy can take several hits, and is immune to pain or exhaustion. They do bleed out and die, but they are hardened and don't quit until dead. Head shots work best.

We drove through the night until we hit the Hairatan road. We decided our best chance was to get to the Afghan Army base at the border so we traveled north. This truck is out of fuel and instead of splitting the precious fuel we have left we have decided to abandon this vehicle and use what we have to get to the border. We have almost no water left, and only a little food. We haven't seen anyone or heard anyone on the radio for at least 24 hours.

If you find this note please give it to the nearest NATO ISAF military units for a reward.

Signed,

SFC Turner

Brad read the note and walked back to Méndez and Eric. He handed the note to Méndez and watched him read it silently.

"Oh shit, this is bad, man," Méndez mumbled.

"Let's get back in the truck. I need to think," Brad said. They mounted the MRAP and sat quietly while Brad stared at the note.

"Sergeant, there is a haboob coming from up the road," said Cole.

Brad looked up. Seeing the large gathering sandstorm, he ordered Cole to close the hatch.

As the sandstorm got close, Brad looked at it through his binos and saw that it wasn't a storm at all, but a mob of at least a thousand coming down the Hairatan road.

"Shut off the engine, Henry, everyone lock the doors and get down," Brad yelled.

"What are we doing Sergeant? Why don't we run?" asked Henry.

"We don't have time. I think if we are quiet they will go past us. They didn't touch the abandoned MRAP. If we are lucky and keep our mouths shut, they will go right by."

The mob hit them, but not with the violence of their first encounter. They didn't seem to move as fast when they weren't chasing prey. They walked quickly but not at the speed they'd seen earlier. They were clumsy, and Brad could hear them bumping against the heavy armored vehicle. A couple even climbed up and over the truck, but none looked inside the darkened interior. It took fifteen minutes for the herd to pass and another twenty minutes for the stragglers to go by.

Brad slowly lifted himself from the vehicle floor. The inside of the truck had gotten extremely hot with the windows closed and the AC turned off. He raised his head up and looked as best he could in a 360 to make sure they were alone. When he was certain, he gave the all clear and told Henry to fire up the engine as he opened his window. He looked outside and saw that the mob had made a wide path in the sand, littered with pieces of clothing and shoes.

They seemed to march with purpose and didn't quit. Brad wondered how they decided where to go.

He got out of the MRAP and walked among some of the things dropped by the mob. He leaned down to pick up a shoe when he heard the shuffling sounds of something approaching. He looked back at his truck and saw his crew signaling for him to get to cover. But it was too late. The thing had already spotted him and started moving directly at him. Lucky for Brad this thing had a gimped leg; it looked like it had a blown-out knee by the way it dragged its foot behind it.

"Sergeant! Shoot it!" Cole yelled from the turret.

"No, hold your fire. If we shoot with the mob still that close they might come back for us," Brad answered.

He pulled out his karambit knife and dropped into a fighter's stance, waiting for the crazy to get within range. When it got close enough it lunged at Brad head first, which was a mistake, as Brad was an experienced wrestler. He grabbed it by the hair on the top of its head and buried the karambit deep into the side of its neck. He thought that would be the end of it, but the thing continued its lunge, grabbing at Brad's legs. Brad had to make a deep sprawl so he could land on top of it and keep his legs out of range. He yanked out the knife and plunged it deep into the base of the thing's skull. This time the creature went limp and settled onto the ground.

Brad got back to his feet and wiped his blade off on the thing's pants. He noticed his hands were shaking; he was shocked at the strength of the creature, and that it didn't quit, even with five inches of steel in its jugular.

He dropped to the ground and sat there for a second before dry heaving into the sand next to him. When he looked up, his men were standing around him and looking down at what he had just killed. Brad rolled the man over and saw a middle-aged Asian man, not like the typical Afghan they ran into around this area. He reached into its jacket pocket and found a tattered wallet. The identification card wasn't in English, but he recognized the papers from his time earlier working at the border.

Brad folded the papers and put them in his pocket.

"What is it Sergeant? What did you find?" asked Cole.

"Nothing guys, do a quick check on the truck and make sure nothing was damaged. Méndez, help me look this thing over some more," Brad answered.

When the others moved away, Brad told Méndez that he was sure the papers were Uzbekistan identification documents. "What do you think that means, Sergeant?" Méndez asked.

"Well, I hope it doesn't mean that this has spread into Uzbekistan. I hope it doesn't mean that the border post has been lost. I hope it doesn't mean we're screwed. Méndez, I need you to help me keep this from the men until we get to Hairatan. I need these guys to stay focused," Brad said.

"I think you have a point, Sergeant," agreed Mendez. "I won't say shit till we know for sure what we are looking at."

Brad and Méndez walked back to the truck and got on board. "Let's move out, Henry," Brad said in a low voice. Henry pulled the vehicle forward and around the abandoned MRAP in the middle of the road. They passed a sign that said 'Hairatan 15km'. "We will be there soon guys, just stay sharp," Brad said.

"If there is anything left there. I mean, you saw that pack of them. They came from where we're headed. What do we expect to find there?" Eric said.

"Just keep your head on straight and worry about that when we get there," ordered Brad.

The road to Hairatan passed through the arid desert before it moved near the Amu Darya River. The landscape slowly began to lose the tan beige of the desert and they saw hints of green. As they got closer to the river they passed an occasional mud hut. They continued on as the road turned to the east and skirted the river; they could see it below them on the left. Still, they saw no signs of life. As they got closer to Hairatan they began to see more and more abandoned vehicles. Some looked as if they had been trampled; others were rolled over and their windshields were shattered.

Henry carefully navigated around the broken and battered vehicles, but the congested road soon became almost impassable. Henry eased the vehicle to the shoulder and prepared to go off road to skirt a large bus that had broken down and was blocking the left lane. Henry pushed the accelerator and the MRAP began to climb the embankment.

"No! Stop!" Cole yelled from the gunner's hatch.

Henry hit the brakes and the vehicle slammed forward, then stopped.

"What is it?" Brad asked.

Cole pointed forward. Brad opened his door and stood in its frame to get a better vantage point. Ahead and off to the side, he saw the missing MRAP.

It looked like they had attempted the same maneuver to get around the bus. They must have climbed the embankment and tried to skirt around the bus, but lost traction and slid into the deep ditch at the other side of the bus. The MRAP and ditch were out of Henry's view, and he never would have seen them until it was too late.

"Back up, Henry," Brad said.

They all got out and wearily approached the disabled MRAP.

Just like the abandoned truck on the road, this truck also had its mounted gun removed. Brad took that as a good sign. When they got closer they could see that the crew had spent a considerable amount of time trying to recover the vehicle. They saw spare tires and cables tied and propped under the MRAP in every position imaginable to try and right it. There was no sign of the crew, and this time there was no note. It looked like they must have lost the fight and were forced to abandon the truck. The vehicle was empty, and they had taken everything removable with them. Brad hoped he wouldn't have to make the same decision.

The bus blocking the road was wedged in tight, and there didn't seem to be any way around it. The other side of the road had a sharp drop off. Brad approached a car near that side and looked inside. The keys were missing and the windshield was smashed out. From the blood spatters on the glass and the hood, it looked like the last owner of the car had been dragged through it. Brad reached through the window, put the car in neutral, and started to push it. Méndez picked up on what Brad was doing and leaned into the back of the car. They pushed hard and Brad steered the car out over the edge of the cliff.

Brad instructed Henry to follow them down the now cleared up lane. Cole stayed in the turret to provide cover, while Eric and Méndez helped Brad push vehicles over the side. It was hard work but eventually they made it through the pileup and the MRAP had room to maneuver again. Eric got back inside the truck while Brad and Méndez elected to ride on the hood.

They approached the outer edge of the city of Hairatan and came to a fork in the road. Brad instructed Henry to stick to the north fork which would take them along the river and to the Afghan Army post. As they travelled, Brad started to make out the steel girded Friendship Bridge which connected Afghanistan to Uzbekistan, an important trade route and path for military shipments. He wasn't happy that he could already tell the bridge looked heavily damaged, and some vehicles even appeared to be burning.

He knew the head of the bridge on the Afghan side was barricaded so people couldn't just drive up to it. Brad instructed Henry to move the MRAP up onto the railway bed that ran parallel to the road and around the barriers. The MRAP slowly climbed the railroad tracks and eased into the customs station. Strangely, there were no train cars, and the inspection station was eerily quiet. Brad and Méndez dismounted with Eric while Cole stood watch in the turret. Brad asked Henry to kill the engine while they listened.

They heard them before they saw them: four males and a female running towards them from down on the far side of the barricade. They were running along the fence trying to make their way to the gate so they could get around and at the soldiers. Brad watched them as they crashed through the gate and began coming up the embankment. He looked through his red dot sight and took aim at a large man in a yellow shirt leading far out in front. He pulled the trigger and hit him in the chest with a three-round burst. The man fell and the others ran over him. Brad told the men to open fire.

They took carefully aimed shots that hit the crazies several times, but they kept coming. "Aim for the head," Brad yelled. And he again aimed for the lead runner, putting the red dot just below his chin and pulling the trigger. He saw his rounds pop through the neck and face of the runner. When he lowered his rifle, all of them were down. They changed out magazines in their M4s and looked around. Off in the distance, the man in yellow he had initially shot was getting back to his feet and making his way towards them.

They stared at the man in awe. Brad raised his rifle and placed the dot over the man's heart and pulled the trigger. Yellow Shirt spun around and fell, but rolled back to his belly, got back to his feet and started walking again towards the soldiers. Brad aimed at the man's leg and took a shot. Yellow Shirt's knee buckled and he went into the dirt, but began crawling towards them. They stood, gaping, and watched the man crawl until he was less than ten feet away. Finally Brad placed a shot in Yellow Shirt's head, stopping him.

"What the fuck was that?" Méndez muttered.

Eric walked to the downed man and rolled him over to his back. There were four holes going across the man's chest, two in the abdomen, one in the heart, and one in the lungs. "How is this possible? You shot him three too many times to kill him and he kept going," Eric said.

As they stared at Yellow Shirt, Cole shouted, "Contact right!" Brad spun to see two more figures running towards them. The two crazies were wearing border guard uniforms. At first Brad thought maybe help had arrived, but he could hear their high-pitched whines.

Without instruction, they raised their rifles and dropped the former guards with well-aimed shots to the grapes. They walked over to the downed men; one of them had a gaping wound on his shoulder; the other was missing a good portion of his neck.

"It looks like whatever this is, it keeps them alive. Look at these wounds; these guys should have been immobile," Eric exclaimed.

"It's definitely not good Eric. I don't know what to say right now," Brad answered.

Méndez rolled one of the guards over and found a Makarov pistol in the man's holster. "No sense in leaving this," Méndez said as he tucked the pistol into his body armor.

"Back to the truck, guys, I'm sure this shooting attracted a lot of attention," said Brad.

Henry drove the truck deeper into the border post compound. Eventually he found a spot behind some shipping containers. He found a horseshoe stack of containers and backed the MRAP and trailer in nicely so they couldn't be snuck up on from behind, but they still had a good view to the front. It wasn't a perfect place to defend against an armed enemy, but it was good tactics against the crazies they were facing.

Once the engine was shut down they listened intently for any sounds that they had been discovered, but it was quiet. Now that they were in the city they did hear the occasional scream and some sporadic gunfire in the distance, but for the most part the compound appeared to be secured. Brad set up a watch schedule and told his guys to try and get some rest.

It was mid-day and the sun was high in the sky. The inside of the MRAP heated up quickly with the engine and cooling systems shut down. Brad knew the conditions were not ideal. He allowed the men to dismount from the truck and try to cool off in the shade under the vehicle; however, the heat still rolled off the pavement and radiated from the vehicle and shipping containers. Brad climbed to the top of the truck and used his binoculars to try and scout the area. He had a good open view of the compound, and could see the warehouse buildings off in the distance. Most of the fence still looked to be in place, and the warehouse doors were all closed and secure.

Brad decided to take a small foot patrol to find a better hide; they couldn't sit here in the hundred degree heat and cook. He told Cole and Eric to suit up and be ready to move in fifteen minutes, leaving Méndez in charge of the vehicle. They packed their gear and put on their knee and elbow pads. Because they were no longer facing a traditional enemy, it was decided to drop the heavy bullet-stopping ceramic plates from their vests, and to also close up the neck and shoulder protectors on their body armor. Designed to protect soldiers from shrapnel and road side bombs, they hoped the Kevlar fabric would now prove useful against the rabid mobs they were faced with.

Cole crept out around the container and led the way on point. He walked slowly and stuck close to the edge of the containers. He stopped often to listen and to look at far off objects through his rifle's advanced optics. The enemy didn't appear to be particularly cunning, but they had managed to sneak up on them more than once, and they didn't want that to happen without the safety of the MRAP. Quickly, yet silently, the patrol moved until they were within a football field's distance from the first warehouse. Cole put his fist in the air and waved them down to the ground. Brad crawled forward and used his binos to look at the building.

It was made entirely of cinderblock, and appeared to be new; probably part of the International Security Force reconstruction efforts. The building had a large overhead door in its center and a smaller door to its right. A row of windows lined the very top of the building, likely for venting and to let in daylight. They watched and waited for a good twenty minutes to make sure they were alone before they got to their feet. One at a time they bounded across the distance and stacked up on the warehouse door. Brad reached across and tried the handle. It turned easily in his hand and he was relieved to find the door unlocked. He held up three fingers and dropped them one at a time. He swiftly and professionally entered the room to clear everything within their view.

A large empty bay with rows of shelving filled the back wall. To the right, he found a block of offices and a set of stairs that led to a loft with more office space above them. They took their time in clearing the row of offices one by one, and then went up the flight of stairs to confirm the building was empty. At the top of the stairs Brad signaled for them to stop, and put a finger over his lips. He pointed to a desk where he could see a foot sticking from behind a half wall of a cubicle. Brad silently un-holstered his M9 pistol and slowly cut the corner, allowing him to slowly see what was on the other side without making himself a target.

He peeked into the cubicle and saw a man sitting with his face down on his desk. The back of his head had a large exit hole and his brains were still running down the back wall of his cube.

"Well, looks like someone decided to check out early," Brad whispered.

The man still clutched an S&W Sigma pistol, which Brad grabbed and put it in his pack. Now that the building was clear, he called the MRAP on his headset and informed Méndez that the warehouse was safe, and they would be returning. He told him to be ready to move when they got there. Cole and Eric tried the large overhead door and found it operational; even though the power was out, the manual chain system still seemed to work fine.

Once the team was together, they quietly guided the truck back to the warehouse and pulled it and the trailer through the large overhead door. They parked the vehicle, then started setting up a defensive perimeter. The warehouse only had the two entrances: the small entry door and the large overhead. Brad placed a metal clip on the chain and pulley system of the door to prevent anyone from being able to raise it. The bolt lock on the entry door didn't appear to work, so they pulled it tight and secured it with some rope and zip ties, fastening it as tightly as they could. It wouldn't keep a determined individual out, but it would give them warning if anyone tried to get in.

Brad asked the men to unload and get a good inventory of everything in the trailer and onboard the vehicle. Then Brad and Méndez went into the office spaces and tried to search for anything to give them a means of working communication. The phones were dead, and the power was out, so all of the computers were also offline. Méndez came back around the corner holding a cell phone he had pulled from the man's pocket in the upstairs cubicle. The phone had full bars, but every number he dialed gave a busy signal. They had already tried the radios in the MRAP several times with no response, so it appeared they were alone and without any comms.

Méndez spotted a ladder well that went up to the roof. After climbing it, they saw they had an immense view of the entire compound and some of the city (most of which was burning). They could see a mass of the crazies moving down a city street far to the east. There wasn't much to see across the river; the bridge was congested and blocked. It looked like the Uzbeks might have attempted to destroy the bridge. There was a large hole in the concrete on the Uzbek side. There wasn't much to look at on the far side of the river, and no movement could be detected. They searched the horizon and no aircraft could be seen, and no streaking of smoke that usually crisscrossed the sky.

It was decided that the roof would make the best watch station so they moved one of the machine guns and a sniper rifle up to the top. The roof was lined by a three-foot wall that made staying in cover easy. They chose a spot in a corner facing the gate to place the machine gun and sniper rifle. Brad put Henry and Eric on the first watch and instructed Méndez and Cole to start doing maintenance on the MRAP and the rest of the equipment. He didn't know how long they would have to hide in their new home. He wanted to make sure everything worked if they had to leave in a hurry.

They moved the body of the man from the cubicle downstairs and laid him under a tarp in a far corner of the warehouse. The men laid out their gear and bed rolls in the loft. There was a small bathroom in the downstairs offices and the water was still running, so they filled every container they could find.

They took advantage of the running water to take much needed sponge baths. It was hard to remember how long they had been on the move. The two nights of running and hiding in the desert had taken a toll on them. Brad thought it would be best to just let the men rest for the remainder of the day. They locked up tight and settled in.

Brad was sitting on the roof in the small sniper's position they had put together. As night came, the quiet of the city ceased. Whatever was roaming the streets seemed to get more animated after sunset. Brad wondered if the things worked better in the cooler night air. Whatever it was, they were definitely moving and making a racket.

Through the night vision scope he could see far into the city, and he watched small engagements between local residents and the crazed mobs. He saw a small car speeding through the streets. It would stop and pick people up, then drive off again. Occasionally the car would skid to a stop, and men with AK47s would jump out and spray sporadic fire at the mobs before they would jump back into the car and speed off again. *At least someone is fighting them*, Brad thought.

He scanned the perimeter of the compound and saw the pedestrian gate where the crazies they had engaged earlier had come through, as well as the railroad entrance that they'd driven the MRAP through. He cursed himself for not securing those gates. It would have to be a priority tomorrow. There were hundreds of shipping containers stacked around the customs yard. *Hopefully, they are filled with food and water, but not likely,* he chuckled to himself. Tomorrow they would find out.

A flare to the north of the city got his attention, and apparently the attention of the crazies as well. All over the city, he could see them lift their heads to the sky and run towards the light. "Note to self, don't use flares," Brad said under his breath.

He strained his eyes through the scope to try and see who had launched the flare, but he couldn't make out the distant figures. Suddenly, he heard the report of heavy weapons, M240B and M249 light machine guns, the telltale sound of M4s, and the crack of M67 frag grenades.

Eric looked up from the machine gun he had been manning on the corner of the building. "Hey! It's a rescue; those are our guys out there!"

Brad put down the rifle and picked up the more powerful binoculars; even though they didn't have the night vision of the scope, he didn't need it with the illumination of the battle. He could see what was happening, and it wasn't rescue forces. "I think I found SFC Turner," he said.

The missing men from the ambush were putting up a fight in a walled-in villa on the south edge of the city. They were putting out an impressive wall of fire, but unfortunately, every crazy in the city within earshot was stopping in its tracks and heading towards the commotion. "Shit, they need to get out of there! They can't hold off that many," Brad said.

"Let's take the MRAP, we can get them out," yelled Eric.

"There is no way, we would never break through that mob, and even if we did we wouldn't be able to open the doors or be able to man our turret. This is fucked," Brad answered.

The mob crashed against the large gate of the walled villa; the men fired down at them from elevated positions, tossing grenades into the crowd.

The mobs would break, and then rebound with more force than before. The wall began to give and Brad watched the soldiers fall back to the house, then reappear on the roof. He saw the flash of a claymore explode in the courtyard. When he looked back only two soldiers remained on the roof. He observed the rest sneak out of the back corner of the building and over a wall. The men on the roof dropped smoke and frag grenades into the crowd. Brad lost sight of them in the smoke and the gunfire ceased. All he heard was the distant roar of the mob.

"Man, I hope they got out," Eric muttered.

Brad scanned all around the building but he could find no evidence of the soldiers. The mob had taken the villa and they were now on the roof in a frenzy. They were attacking each other and screaming. It was hours before they calmed down and faded back into the city streets.

The screaming and occasional gunfire continued through the night and went silent just before dawn. Brad didn't sleep at all and he was sure his men didn't get much rest either.

At first light, he sent Eric and Cole out to secure the gates while Henry and Méndez provided cover from the small nest on the roof. Brad went down to the offices and started to rummage through the desks. Most of the paperwork wasn't in English, and he couldn't make shit out of the gibberish on the page. But finally he found a clipboard with what he was looking for—a manifest from the rail companies. He could make sense of some of the brand names and the lot numbers. He hoped it would help them in breaking down some of the shipping containers. He wrote down a few numbers on his notepad that looked like they belonged to produce or beverage companies.

Armed with a pair of bolt cutters and two duffel bags, he headed out of the safety of the warehouse with Cole providing rear security. They moved to the stack of shipping containers, trying to decipher the numbering system from his notes and connect it to what they were seeing on the ground.

"Well, it doesn't look like they made this easy for us, nothing is in order," Brad whispered to Cole.

They decided to give up on the scavenger hunt and just start opening containers. Brad provided security while Cole cut the locks and seals on one of the large doors, and he helped him swing it open.

The inside was filled with boxes of nails and bolts, and all types of construction fasteners.

"Dammit! Strike one I guess," Cole mumbled.

They moved on and tried another four containers before they opened one filled completely with cases of energy drinks. "Shit, looks like we won't be dying tired," Brad joked and they both laughed. They dumped two cases of the drinks into a duffle bag and marked the location on a map Brad had drawn.

The last container in the row was filled with canned goods. They couldn't read the labels to know what it was, exactly, but at least it was food. They marked the location, filled both bags, and headed back to the warehouse.

Back at their hideout, Méndez used his utility knife to cut open one of the cans of food. They found a small metal pot in one of the back offices and built a small fire made with pieces of broken furniture. He tilted the can and its contents plopped into the pot. "Fuck bro, that stinks. Man, you sure this ain't dog food?" Méndez said.

"I don't think so. It has some goofy ass kid's face on the can. If it was dog food it would show a dog," answered Cole.

"Well damn, man, this shit is awful. No wonder Afghans are always pissed off if they be eating on this slop. Whatever happened to Chunky soup? How do you fuck up soup? Sarge, you sure we can't just eat the MREs?" Eric griped.

"No, we need to save them, and I want to keep the light stuff loaded in the packs and on the truck in case we need to bug out. This is what we got so dump in a couple more cans and appétit!" answered Brad.

They ate in silence. After a minute, Méndez reached down to open another can; everyone looked up at him. "You know, once you get over the shit taste, it really ain't so bad," Méndez chuckled. All the men laughed together.

"I bet that stuff is going to give you the shits too," Eric blurted out.

"So what's the plan anyhow, Sergeant?" Henry asked suddenly, killing the jovial mood.

"Well for now I'm thinking rest, fortify, and build up our resources. After that I am pretty wide open to suggestions," Brad answered back. "I mean, we are far away from our area of operations; our command is gone; and our home base is destroyed. The only hint that anyone even knows we're here is that UAV we saw two days ago. And they might not even know who we are."

"Do you think Sergeant Turner got out last night?" Eric asked.

"I don't know, buddy, but if anyone could it was him. Remember they escaped the ambush and they made it this far. Plus they chose to go to the city and not lock up tight in this warehouse," said Brad. "They have the confidence and training to make it, so I'm not giving up on them yet. I've patrolled this way before and there really isn't shit past Hairatan. Beyond the city the road fizzles out. There are some villages and farms going out along the river, but there's no bridge. Eventually we will have to make a choice: to try and cross the bridge into Uzbekistan on foot or head back into Afghanistan. We could try for Mazari Sharif, it's about a half day's patrol to the south, but after seeing this place, I got a bad feeling about that also," Brad finished.

"My vote is stay put for a few days and see if communications come back up," Méndez said. They all came to an agreement to wait things out for a while. Cole and Eric moved back up the ladder to the roof to start the evening watch.

Brad had settled into his bedroll up on the loft of the warehouse. *Damn!* he thought, *if I knew we weren't going back to base that night I would have brought my pillow*. He smiled to himself and placed the S&W pistol he'd found earlier by his side.

Once he stopped moving, exhaustion took over and he drifted into a dreamless sleep. He felt a hand grab and shake his foot. Brad jumped up, grabbing the pistol and pointing it into Cole's shocked face. "Oh shit, my bad, Sergeant," uttered Cole. "I shouldn't have been so quiet."

Brad lowered the pistol and relaxed. "What is it Cole?"

"Sergeant, you need to get up top. Something you need to see," Cole answered.

Brad sent Cole ahead and he stopped to put on his boots and his vest. He looked at his watch. *Damn, it's only been two hours*. He climbed the ladder and settled into the nest with Eric and Cole. "What do we got, fellas?" he whispered.

"Over there Sergeant, just past the fence in that little building," Cole said, pointing with his finger. Brad picked up the binos and looked down towards the building.

"I don't see anything, guys," he said.

"Just wait, Sergeant. There it is," Eric said, pointing. Brad saw three flickers of a red light followed by three long flashes and three more flickers.

"Oh shit guys, that's Morse code, someone is signaling. But who are they talking to?" Brad whispered.

"It's got to be us, Sergeant. We're the only ones up here," Eric replied.

"Go wake up Henry, he's good with this nerdy shit, and grab the red lens flashlight off my bag," Brad said.

Moments later Henry was crouched in the sniper's nest with the flashlight and a pen and paper. After checking his work, he finally spoke. "They said '*we are two U.S.*', and they want to come into the compound."

"Well ask them who they are," snapped Brad.

After another set of exchanges Henry spoke again. "They just say, '*we are two U.S., request permission to enter your perimeter*'."

"What do you think, guys?" Brad asked.

The men looked puzzled that Brad was asking for advice, it wasn't typically his way.

"Come on guys! Cut me a break, this isn't exactly a military op any more. I'm open to suggestions."

"I say let them in, Sergeant. Why would they tell us they are coming if they were up to no good?" Cole said.

Brad smiled. "You make a good point, Cole. Henry, tell them to come in but stay in our line of sight."

They watched as the two men broke cover of the building and walked in a slow crouch to the fence.

Brad thought they would circle around to the perimeter gate. But without making a sound they quickly cut through to the inside, turned around, repaired the fence, and disappeared into the shadows. A moment later, they heard a tapping at the downstairs door.

Brad looked over the roof wall and saw the two dark figures huddled at the door. He turned, and he and Cole rushed down the ladder, waking up Méndez. With his pistol in his hand, Brad undid the bindings on the door and let it slowly open outward. The two men hurried inside and closed the door behind them. The man in front dropped the dark hood he had been wearing, gave a toothy, bearded grin, and extended his hand to Brad.

"U.S. Navy SEALS, we're here to get you out," he laughed. Brad didn't return the handshake and instead just stared at the man. "Why so stern, Sergeant? Just fucking with you. We've been watching you guys the better part of two days. It's good to be inside with you. It's not a lot of fun out there in the city," the man said.

"So who are you guys? Where did you come from?" Brad asked.

"Damn kid, where are your manners? Getting all personal and not even offering a guest a beverage," the man replied.

"Shit, my fault," said Cole, laughing and holding up a couple of cans of energy drink.

They all chuckled and moved towards the interior of the warehouse. Méndez secured the door and followed them inside. Brad looked the men over; they were solid but not large. Both had overgrown beards and they wore an arrangement of camouflage. Instead of issue boots, they were wearing civilian-style hiking shoes.

Both men carried huge packs and an assortment of weapons. The chatty man carried a large scoped rifle and had a suppressed MP5 strapped to the top of his pack. His partner carried a scoped M14 as well as a silenced MP5, and they both had large handguns at their hips. They wore dark-patterned cargo pants and large, dark-and-tan-splattered hooded jackets—they definitely blended into the terrain here in northern Afghanistan. The man saw the pot and asked if they had any more.

"Tastes like shit," answered Brad, "but suit yourself."

Méndez smiled, reached over to stir the coals on the fire, and started to open a couple of cans of the Afghan slop.

"So you care to make a proper introduction now?" Brad asked.

"Yeah, sorry about that," the man laughed. "I'm Chief Sean Rogers. This is my partner Petty Officer Brooks. We really *are* SEALs," he smiled, "but we sure as hell ain't in any condition to get you all out."

"How did you get here? What are you doing all the way up here?" Eric asked.

The chief began to speak. "Well, we been up here for a week now. We started about a hundred miles from here; been in the city for three days now. You guys were smart to hole up here. There ain't shit but bad news out on those streets. We saw your Army brothers last night making all that noise. It was real John Wayne of them picking that fight, but also really fucking stupid. We've been watching you guys, trying to make sure you weren't fucking stupid too. We don't like to make camp with stupid people."

Sean paused to open the can of energy drink and he gulped it down, spilling some on his beard. "That shit done yet?" he asked, digging a canteen cup out of his pack and handing it to Méndez. Brooks dug out a similar cup and handed it over; Méndez poured the contents of the pot between the two cups and handed them back.

"Damn, you weren't lying! This does taste like shit," Brooks said, and all the men laughed.

"So Chief, you were saying how you got here," Brad said.

"Oh yeah. Well, we were a ways north of here in Teremez doing a little recon and trying to close out some leads, when we were told our pickup was going to be delayed. Later we were told it was canceled and we should try and make our way to the base at Hairatan. And yeah, that's pretty much when the world went to shit," Sean answered.

"Wait a minute," Brad asked. "Teremez? You were operating in Uzbekistan? And what do you mean the world went to shit? This thing is everywhere?"

"Well Sergeant, I guess I can't say for certain, but we know for a fact things are bad out there."

"Fuck yeah they are!" Brad yelled. "I lost my entire company yesterday, so will you stop fucking around and tell us what's going on!"

"Stand down Sergeant! You think you're the only one that has lost people this week? I went to Teremez with six men; Brooks is all that I have left. If you'll sit back down, I'll try and explain." Sean scooped up a mouthful of the slop, swallowed, then continued. "About two months ago we lost an embassy in Yemen, you may have heard about it."

"Oh yeah, that was fucked up! They got rushed by protestors; the ambassador was killed. Al Qaeda, right?" Eric added.

"Well, something like that," Sean answered. "What the people don't know is that we had four former SEALs assigned to protect that ambassador, and a contingent of Marine guards. Now what sort of protestors can take down that kind of muscle?"

"What are you getting at, Chief?" Brad asked.

"Well Sergeant, we now believe that was a test shot. We think the crowd in Yemen was infected. They tore through the embassy residence, walked through a wall of gunfire, and took everything out. The reason CNN showed the smoking rubble the next day and blamed it on mortars and rockets is because the Marine commander onsite ordered a C130 gunship to rain fire on his own position. He knew the ambassador was already dead and he had watched one of his men turn in the three-hour battle. That Marine captain stopped the spread," Sean said. He paused to take another huge gulp of his energy drink. And went on to explain what they had found.

"We aren't sure where it comes from, but we know that Al Qaeda found a way to make a weapon out of it. The nerds at the CDC call it *primalis rabia* or primal rage. It affects the brain, somehow protects it. You can stop the heart. You can shoot them through the lungs and the brain will still function for hours. It spreads through blood. A spit in the eye won't do it, but get infected fluids into your blood and you're screwed. Once a victim is infected, he slips into a coma, and then gets a fever. The heat of the fever seems to cause irreversible brain damage, then for reasons they can't figure out yet, the brain reboots. When the victim wakes up they are feral.

"The longer the person is infected the harder they are to bring down. Recently infected ones can still be killed with a shot to the heart. Those infected for over forty-eight hours, good luck, only extreme trauma to the body seems to bother them. After ninety-six hours, the brain is fully protected and nothing will kill them but a critical brain hit. They move in packs like wolves, and they will attack on sight.

"The attack in Yemen put them on our radar. But we still didn't know how to react until twelve days ago. A man code-named Asim walked into a field office in Pakistan. He said that there was a major global attack planned by the Sons of Bin Laden. Asim carried a special ink pen, but instead of ink it contained the virus. It was a brutal method of transmission. All you do is stab yourself with the pen, click the button, and bam! You are infected. In the lab it took anywhere from two to six hours for the victims to reboot. Asim said there were over one hundred pens made and distributed globally. He only knew the locations of those in his cell and he gave them up. He was supposed to walk into a crowded mosque in Karachi and infect himself, then wait for it to take hold. Asim came to us instead."

"What happened next?" Brad asked.

Sean continued, "Well, my team was sent into Teremez. Asim had fingered two members of his cell who had orders to infect themselves simultaneously on different edges of the city. One tango at the airport and another tango at a popular park. We set up and staked out both locations, but things got difficult; things went wrong. I went with Brooks to the park; we watched for Tango One all afternoon. We had a good description of him but everyone that day seemed to look alike. Toward the end of the day, we spotted a suspect and took him down in a men's room. We found the pen on him. Tango One didn't want to answer our questions. We needed to know how to find Tango Two. He didn't want to cooperate so we quickly eliminated him from the equation and turned our attention to the airport.

"The rest of my guys were set up in the international terminal. They just had too many suspects. They tried to find people sleeping or in the coma phase, but no dice. It happened quickly and without warning. In the smaller terminal Tango Two went crazy. They heard it over their police scanners. The local police were responding and by the time my men got there, they had already put down Tango Two.

"But therein lay the problem. Tango Two managed to scratch, bite, and claw a number of people before he went down. We didn't even know how many because a number of them fled or went home after the incident. The Uzbek police thought they were dealing with just another insane person and didn't buy our story. Even when we notified Interpol they didn't care to listen. The Uzbeks were more concerned about us operating within their border than a possible epidemic about to explode on them.

"So victims go home, they feel sick, they go to bed, they wake up, and they attack their families, neighbors. Simultaneously all over Teremez, we were tracking at least fifteen outbreaks; by morning we heard of ninety more, then it just snowballed from there. By the second day the city was in flames. We called for extraction, but they told us we needed to hang tight. See, Teremez was just one attack; this was going on everywhere and somehow it had even gotten into a few of our larger bases.

"Bagram and Kandahar were lost quickly, and within twelve hours we had a complete loss of combat readiness in theater. All bases were locked down, NATO recalled all of its troops, the U.S. followed suit. That was chaos in itself, there just weren't enough birds to move them, and with that they were battling the primal virus at the same time. Gentlemen, it's pretty safe to say it was a huge cluster fuck. We stayed in contact with Kabul through that first night, but they were in bad shape and we eventually lost comms. The last message to us was to try and make it to the border."

"What about your men? Where's the rest of your team?" Eric asked.

"Dead. Getting out of that city was hell. It's not like here, this place is small. Teremez on Day Two? You're talking close to a hundred thousand of those fucking things on the streets," Brooks said. "Chief and I got separated from the team. We were providing overwatch while they moved on ahead. They were surrounded and quickly overrun. It's a fucked up world out there. They didn't have a chance; in numbers it's like fighting a tidal wave."

"What about the States, Chief? What's going on at home?" Brad asked.

"We don't know. Honest answer? Last update we got, there were no attacks in the U.S., but Mexico and Canada were nearly lost. Moscow, Paris, and London all got hit hard. Germany was attacked but they were holding," answered Sean. "Our sat phone died two days ago, and our radios haven't worked in three. Boys, we are in the dark."

Brad then told the SEALs their story, how they'd lost communications during their patrol to the village, about the mobs, how they had barely escaped and made it to Hairatan.

"So what do we do Chief? What was your plan B?" asked Brad.

Sean let out a sigh. "Plan B? Shit, son, we are already on plan C, hell, we are off the page."

They were interrupted by the sounds of gunfire and they all climbed the ladder to the roof. The small car was back, repeating the acts of last night. They watched it stop while two men jumped out and fired away at the mob until it was within fifty meters, then they jumped back in their car and sped away.

"Ha! That's just Junayd, don't worry about him," chuckled Brooks.

"What's so funny?" Brad asked.

"Oh Junayd, he's a local Taliban boss. We bumped into him crossing the river. Well, we saved his ass actually. We gave him our car and those rifles he's using," said Brooks. "He is determined to take back his city."

"You armed the Taliban?" questioned Eric incredulously.

"Hell yeah we did, if they are keeping the primal bastards busy then they stay the hell away from us, and the enemy of my enemy is my friend, right?" answered Sean.

"What about the other army unit, Sergeant Turner and his guys?" Cole asked.

"Yeah, they are out there. We watched them escape, but for some reason they don't like to lay low. Not sure how long they will last without instruction," said Sean. "They took up residence in a two-story building on the edge of the city. I'm sure they aren't as comfy as you all are in here."

"Well then we need to get to them, we can't leave them hanging out there, Chief," said Brad.

"Tomorrow son, tomorrow. But for now? Chief needs his sleep. Besides, them things are too active at night, we would never make it. So how 'bout you guys show us where we can bed down," said Sean.

The next morning they did maintenance on their vehicle and equipment. Cole and Henry made a run to the shipping containers to resupply their stash of Afghan slop and energy drinks. Brad showed Sean the supplies they had on hand.

"You guys have done a good job here, Sergeant, you probably have more ammo than anyone within a hundred miles," Sean said.

"Well, we took everything we could. We have a few extra weapons too, but the MRAP is our baby right now. I don't think we would have escaped the mob at Bremmel without it," replied Brad.

"Yeah she's nice, but she's loud and will attract attention. I'm surprised you didn't get a mob following you right into this fence; you guys got lucky."

"So what's the plan to get Sergeant Turner and his guys?" Brad asked.

"Well, first put this on your M4," Sean said as he handed Brad a threaded suppressor for his rifle. "They are attracted to noise; this will help."

They waited until the sun was high in the sky; that's when the crazies were the least active. Brad left Méndez in charge of the men and the warehouse before he moved out with the SEALs through the compound gate. They were fast, and quiet. Brad was in great shape but the SEALs made him feel like a bumbling idiot as he struggled to keep up with them. They hugged the walls of the buildings, ducked behind abandoned vehicles, and sometimes tucked into alleys to avoid a wandering primal. But the Chief was right; they were less active during the hot midday than they were at night.

As they turned a corner, Brooks put his fist in the air and a finger to his lips. Brad was thankful for the new suppressor attached to his M4 as both Sean and Brooks had readied their silenced MP5s in anticipation. Sean took a knee, leaned into a stone wall, and tried to make himself invisible. A group of five crazies were staggering down the street towards them. They were moving slower than they had during the past two days; Brad wondered if that was a symptom. Did they slow down as they aged? The primals stumbled at a curb and looked like a pack of drunks as they navigated themselves over it. Without warning, Brad heard the clacking of metal on metal from the SEALS guns, and all five of the infected dropped to the ground. Brooks whispered, "Clear!" and they started moving again. Brad was amazed at the efficiency with which the SEALS could unleash violence.

They rounded a corner and tucked into a tiny store. Brooks made sure the room was clear, and then they huddled near the window. "It's that two-story building right there," Sean pointed.

"Well, what are we waiting for? Let's go," Brad said.

"We will, but we need you to go first. Make sure they aren't all hopped up and shoot us," added Brooks.

"Oh, good plan I guess," said Brad. "So, you just want me to walk over there and say 'Hi'?"

"Yeah, but the tricky part is to do it quietly, so you're not seen or heard by the primals, and also be careful not to spook your Army boys into whacking you," grinned Sean.

Brooks opened the storefront door and gave Brad a thumbs up. "Good luck," he whispered. Brad just nodded and made his way to the street; he could see the two-story building had all of its windows covered with heavy drapes. He looked to the left and right and saw no one. He walked into the center of the street, held his hands and rifle over his head, and waved them up and down. There was no response from the building. He watched the windows and saw no movement. The edges of the roof revealed nothing, so he moved to the front door.

He stood by the door listening and heard nothing. "Fuck it," he whispered to himself. He reached up a hand and knocked on the heavy wooden door. He heard nothing so he knocked again. Hearing nothing inside, he turned to signal the SEALS just as the door crashed open and a large man with a knife dove at him. "No, no, no, no," Brad yelled. The man stopped his assault with the blade just inches from Brad's face.

"What the fuck are you doing creeping up on us like that?!" shouted the soldier. Brad recognized him as one of the privates from Third Squad.

Before he could answer, the SEALs had rushed across the street and grabbed them.

"Gentlemen? Perhaps we should have this conversation inside? You boys have already made enough noise," Sean said. They all tumbled through the doorway and Sean closed the door behind them.

Brad found himself standing in a long hallway with doors on both sides and a set of stairs leading up at the end.

"Oh hey! It's you, Sergeant Thompson! Sorry about that man, I thought you was one of them things. I wanted to shut it up before he called his buddies," said the private.

"Where is everyone else?" asked Brad.

"Oh yeah, they're all in the basement. We been sleeping during the day and we all stand watch at night when they go nuts out there. If one of you wants to watch the door, I'll take you down there," answered the private. Brooks nodded to them and dropped his pack. Brad and Sean followed the private down the hall to a heavy steel door.

He knocked on the door and after a minute there was a noise inside and the door cracked open.

"Hey Jones, what you need man?" said the guard.

"We got company. It's Sergeant Thompson, he just showed up knocking on the door."

The guard swung the door open and shook Brad's hand. "Good to see you, Sergeant. We thought you all were dead. Come on down, Sergeant Turner is going to want to talk to you," said the guard, and he led them down the stairs. The cellar was dark and damp; there was very little light, only what came in through the floorboards above their heads.

They made their way into a damp room. Brad saw soldiers sleeping on the floor, and a small area set up as a latrine. They wound through the dark cellar to a smaller entryway. The soldier knocked on the door frame and they heard a grumble from inside.

"What is it," called the voice.

"Sergeant Turner? Sergeant Thompson and some men are here," answered the soldier.

"Huh? What the hell?" A flashlight came on, illuminating the space, and shone into Brad's face. "Well I'll be dammed, it is you! Come on in man. Have a seat," said Sergeant Turner.

Turner lit a small gas lantern and the men made their way into the small room. It was sparsely furnished: nothing but a small table with a map laid out on it, and a handful of chairs. Brad and Sean made their way to the table and took a seat, as Turner hurriedly put on his boots.

"Damn Brad, it's good to see you brother! I thought you guys were dead," Turner said as he slapped him on the back and took a seat next to him. "So who is your friend? Where is the rest of your crew?"

Brad explained the appearance of the SEALS, and that his men were back at the warehouse. He told Turner how they had followed them to Hairatan, and how they had watched their battle the previous night.

"Shit, yeah that was bad. One of the kids got scared and popped that damn flare, and then things went to shit. We lost Smith over it, but we got lucky, the rest of us made it," explained Turner.

"Hey guys, I don't want to be a dick and spoil your reunion, but we only have so much mid-day left. We need to pack up and get moving," said Sean.

"Moving? Move where? We're pretty secure in here; I don't know that we will be moving," quipped Turner.

"Really Sergeant?" snapped Sean. "Low on ammo, your guys are shitting in buckets, I don't see much in the way of food or water, and you're hiding in a cellar. Your soldier here has managed to secure a compound; he has a trailer full of guns and bullets to match, a shipping container of food, running water and flush toilets, but suit yourself. We will be moving in fifteen minutes."

"Whoa! Hold up Chief, I didn't say we wouldn't go. And besides, you make a good point; those buckets are starting to smell the place up. Give me some time to get the men organized and we'll meet you in the hallway upstairs," answered Turner.

Sean and Brad moved back up to the hallway and briefed Brooks on the move back to the warehouse. "I'm not a fan of your Sergeant Turner," Sean said to Brad.

"Don't be too hard on him Chief; he's kept these guys alive for this long; that's got to count for something."

The five soldiers came up the stairs in full packs. They looked beaten and tired, but they said they were ready to get out of the confined cellar. Sean briefed them on how they would move back. There were five of them, so they would move in three teams. Brooks would take point with one, Brad had the middle with two more, and Sean would pick up the rear with the last of them. Sean told them he wanted no firing. If they had to take shots, they were to do it with the suppressed weapons.

"Shit, we don't have any silenced guns," said one of the soldiers.

"Here," said Brooks, handing the soldier a Ruger MK II with a suppressor from his pack. "It's small but it's easy to shoot, and will knock them down if you get them in the nugget. Make sure you hit the head," said Brooks.

Chief reached into his pack and handed his own MK II to Turner. "I'll be wanting that back, Sergeant," he said with a smile.

Once the men familiarized themselves with the pistols, they slowly stepped out the door and made their way into the hot street. Brad followed them and hugged the wall. He had two soldiers right behind him and they mimicked his movements. He waited for Brooks' team to make it past the corner, then Brad bounded forward, looking back to watch Sean and his men fill his previous position. They moved quickly and quietly through the city until they saw Brooks' fist shoot into the air. Brad and his men dropped to the ground and looked for cover. Brad listened intently for a sign of what was going on up ahead.

He heard the *clack, clack* of Brooks' MP5, then the sound of the MK II. Brad took a knee and looked forward as he saw both men walking backwards toward them, firing as fast as they could. Brad got to his feet. He looked through his scope and spotted a group of fifteen to twenty coming at them from the alleyway. Before he could pull the trigger, Sean had already brought his group forward and he was taking quick, aimed shots, thinning the number of the pack headed at them. Turner faced a building on the street and pried its door open, then turned and provided covering fire while the men dropped inside.

Sean and Brooks were the last ones in, and they quickly barricaded the door. The pounding and screaming from the outside was deafening. "Find another exit!" Sean yelled to Brad as they began piling objects against the door. Luckily the door opened out, so the things were pressing it shut as they forced themselves against it.

Brad ran down the long hallway and kicked in an apartment door; as he stepped inside, two crazies came at him from a bedroom. Brad fired at them from the hip with his M4, hitting the first high in the chest and turning it sideways while the second came crashing into him, both of them falling to the ground. Brad was fighting to keep its head and snapping jaws away from him, while the thing scratched and clawed at his body armor. One of the privates followed Brad into the room and quickly ended the crazy with a soccer kick to the head, knocking it loose from Brad. Turning, he then terminated the other one with a burst to the skull from his unsuppressed M4.

The noise of the soldier's rifle made Brad's ears ring, but he pushed through the small apartment and saw a window. He broke the glass with the butt of his rifle and peeked outside. The window opened into an alley on the side of the building. There didn't appear to be a safe way out, but the building across from them had a fire escape with the ladder extended.

Brad gathered the men into the apartment, and told them to get out the window and up the ladder across the alley. He ran back into the hall to find Sean and Brooks finishing the barricading and booby trapping of the door with a claymore mine and trip wire. Brad led the SEALs to the apartment and out the window.

As he suspected, the alley was a dead-end. The open end pointed back to the street where the mob had gathered, but it was also empty. They quickly made their way to the ladder and climbed as high as they could, pulling themselves over the top rung and onto the building's roof, then pulled the ladder up behind them.

Sergeant Turner made his way over to them, announcing that the roof was clear and the access door was secure. With a thundering clap they heard the improvised claymore explode in the building below them. The explosion blasted and partially collapsed the building and blew a cloud of dust into the street out front.

"Well I think they know we're here now," Sean said with a smile.

"No worries though, I don't think anything saw us climb this ladder. If we lay low, they should go back to their nests—in a day or two," Brooks said. Brad frowned at the statement, especially with the sun still high in the sky and his camelback only half full.

Just as Brad was beginning to think it was going to be a long night, they heard the report of AK47s coming from down the street. Brad looked up and over the edge of the roof and saw the small white car. Two men in Arab garb jumped out and began shooting at the mob in front of the destroyed apartment building. When the mob got too close, they jumped back in the car, drove farther down the street, and did it again, effectively leading them away from Brad's position.

"Son of a bitch! It's Junayd!" Brooks said. "Look at that shit; he's clearing the way for us."

Everyone ran to the edge of the roof to look out below; just then a large open-bed truck pulled up in front of the building. A man jumped from the cab and waved frantically at them.

"Well, what do we do, Chief?" asked Brad.

"Looks like he's offering us a ride, rude to turn them down," Sean answered.

Wasting no time, they all made their way back down the ladder. They ran around the corner and jumped into the back of the truck. A small Arab man closed the tailgate behind them and they sped off.

The truck drove quickly down streets, changing directions every block or two, occasionally bouncing a primal off of its large steel bumper. Junayd's men drove for some time until they were sure they had lost any followers. They pulled into a darkened side street with high walls on both sides, far from anyplace Brad recognized. Lifting their heads to look over the high tailgate, they saw the small car pull in behind them. Sean and Brooks got to their feet and leapt to the ground. A large Arab man approached and shook Sean's hand, then embraced Brooks in a bear hug.

"My friends we are even now, you saved me, now I save you," said Junayd.

"You got that right Junayd," said Brooks, smiling at the man, "but we also gave you weapons and a car. It would be really nice of you if you could get us back home, and not just leave us on this street."

"Yes friend, that is a very real possibility, but I need you to also allow my people into your home," said Junayd. "We have seen that you have taken the customs compound; you must take in our people. This city is not safe for them. Take in my people, and we will safely bring you home."

"Well it's not my place to negotiate over, I'm only a guest there, Junayd," answered Sean.

"I see," said Junayd, frowning. "It appears you men will have a long walk home. You should hurry. It will be dark soon."

"Hold up, I think we have room, just get us back to the warehouse and we can work this out," said Brad.

"Wait Brad, we can't trust these people, maybe we should just get out here. I think we're better off on our own," snapped Turner.

Junayd glared at the insult and turned to walk towards the cars. Brad quickly jumped from the bed of the truck and walked over to Junayd. "Junayd, if you get us safely back to the customs compound, I will open my doors to your people. We're all in this fight together now," Brad said, extending his hand.

"Agreed," said Junayd, briefly touching his hand to his heart before grasping Brad's in a tight handshake that quickly turned into a hug.

The ride back to the compound was quiet and uneventful. The vehicles pulled into a narrow ravine that twisted around and behind the customs compound. The large truck lurched to a stop and the small man dropped the tailgate of the truck. The men jumped out, stretched, and looked around. "Go through that hole in the fence," said Junayd, pointing. "If you go through and follow the fence till it ends, you will see the railroad track that will lead you back."

"How do you know that?" asked Brad.

"My cousin and I have been raiding and smuggling things from this customs yard for years. We only asked your permission to stay here to be polite," Junayd said, giving Turner a cold stare. "We have plenty of work fighting those things in the city; we really do not need to be bothered with fighting Americans also. Get back to your warehouse and prepare your men. We will be at your gates shortly after the sun sets."

"Why not wait till tomorrow? You know they are more dangerous at night," asked Brad.

"More dangerous? Yes, but also more predictable. We will use distractions to move the packs where we want them while we deliver the people to you. Be ready for them," Junayd said as he turned and walked back to his car. Shutting the doors, the engines started and the vehicles drove back down the ravine.

Sean walked by and patted Brad on the shoulder; a gesture that didn't go unnoticed by Turner. "You did good Brad, now let's get back to the hooch," said Sean as he stepped to the hole in the fence, gesturing for the men to go through.

They made their way back to the warehouse, and received a warm welcome from the waiting men. Brad briefed them on what had happened and that they were about to receive guests. Sean and a couple of the soldiers cleared the warehouse next door so that it could be set up as lodging for the incoming civilians. Brad took Sergeant Turner on a tour of the compound and helped his men settle into the building. They were happy to see the flush toilets and running water. Brad got Cole started on preparing the evening meal and he told them all to get some rest. As Brad was leaving, Turner called him over.

"You have done well here, Brad, and you did good getting these men here safely. I just want you to know that I won't step on your feet," said Turner. "It seems the world has gone to shit quickly. I don't know where that leaves the military, but I *am* a platoon sergeant and it's going to stay that way. However, I think you have proven yourself, and you should be the acting lieutenant until we come up with something different."

Brad grinned. "I appreciate the gesture, Sergeant, but I don't think you have the authority to give battlefield commissions," he laughed.

"Yeah, you're probably right, but this is the best I got, Brad. It allows me to save face, and will keep the men from getting caught up in a power struggle," responded Turner.

"Well then, sounds good to me. I have work to do, Sergeant, we can talk again later," said Brad.

"Okay buddy, and how 'bout you drop the 'sergeant' shit? We can catch up after I grab some shut eye."

Brad walked outside the warehouse door; he bumped into Sean heading back in the other direction. He explained what had just happened with Turner.

"Well damn, I didn't think the guy had it in him, but I think it was the right decision. I was afraid we wouldn't be able to work together, maybe I was wrong," said Sean.

"Sergeant Turner isn't a bad guy, and he has a lot of combat experience. I trust him."

They were beginning to lose the daylight, so they retreated inside and climbed to the roof. Just as the last bits of sunlight faded, they heard a distant explosion. A fire began to burn, and they heard reports of the AK47 rifles.

"Well there is Junayd, right on time," said Brooks. They could see the primal crazies shifting in the streets and heading towards the racket on the far side of town. Sean grinned when the two flares popped and went high into the sky. "They must have learned that trick from your sergeant," he chuckled.

"Wherever they learned it, it's working. Look at them all, they go to it like mosquitoes to a bug zapper," laughed Cole.

Eric pointed down toward the railroad gate at the front of the compound. "They're here."

Brad stood to look and saw four large flatbed trucks overloaded with people, a few more than he had expected. He watched his men open the gates and guide the overloaded trucks in. They led them all the way down to the empty warehouse. Brad left the roof and made his way down the ladder. When he reached the small convoy of vehicles he was greeted by Junayd with another stiff handshake.

"Thank you my friend," Junayd said. "These people had it very badly out there; I don't think you realize how much safety and security these fences will give them."

Brad watched as his men helped women and children exit the vehicles and enter the warehouse. He moved into the building; it was dark, but they were afraid to turn on any lights while the overhead doors were still open. Sean and his men had laid out cardboard into makeshift mats on the ground for the people to sit on. Brad saw that the warehouse was laid out very similarly to the one they were using.

As he walked, he saw that Eric had converted one of the offices into a medical clinic and he was treating a small child, and others had already started to get in line. The loft area was already occupied by several men and they were carrying their limited supplies up the stairs for safekeeping. Brad looked around and tried to get a count in his head.

"Junayd, you have nearly fifty people here, this will be a lot to feed," Brad said.

"Seventy-two to be exact, and yes it will be a lot, but the city holds resources. Unlike Americans, we know how to live off of this land. We will be fine my friends, shortly my men will return from their mini-Jihad against the monsters in the city. Let's walk so that we may greet them," said Junayd.

As if on cue, they heard the vehicles approaching the gate. While they walked, Brad saw his men working with some of Junayd's men to open the gates and escort in the small car. Once the car pulled in and killed its engine, the small man from before stepped out with four other local fighters. Junayd exchanged words with the man, and then patted him hard on the shoulder while facing Brad.

"This is Hasan, he is my best soldier."

Brad extended his hand and smiled. "I think we almost met earlier today. Thank you for your help, Hasan, and good work getting the people here safely." Hasan smiled as he returned the handshake.

The next several days were spent improving the small camp. The soldiers decided to give up the warehouse space to the civilians and they all moved into a small guardhouse near the gate. Although the guardhouse was smaller, it gave the soldiers privacy and relieved them of the guilt of leaving the families crammed into the single space. They continued to stand watch nightly on the roof of the warehouse in the sniper hide they had set up. With the help of Junayd's men providing distractions so that the noise wouldn't attract the primals, they were able to utilize some of the heavy equipment to move the railroad shipping containers into a large wall. After a few days' work the compound was now ringed in by the large forty-foot-long, ten-foot-high containers.

The men slowly made improvements to the camp's perimeter. After the wall was constructed they started to lose some of the fear of making noise. Any stray primal that moved too close to the compound was quickly terminated with the use of Sean's suppressed sniper rifle. After a week, the camp was fortified. Containers stacked end to end completely enclosed the camp. They had a sliding gate and the men had cut access doors into the containers that held food or other valuable supplies. Brad was extremely happy with the progress made.

Late on the thirtieth night after the outbreak, Brad made his way to the communal fire pit inside his former residence. The warehouse now was divided into small shacks constructed of cardboard and crates salvaged from inside the containers. He saw Junayd with Sean and Brooks off to the side of the fire so he sat next to them. Once he was settled, a smiling young woman handed him a bowl of rice and dried meat. A child handed him an energy drink which made Brad laugh.

"You have done well by these people Brad! They would welcome you into their tribe," said Junayd.

This gave all of the military men a laugh. "I am honored Junayd, really, but this isn't my home. I think there is more for me than this."

Sean gave Brad a serious look. "That's exactly what we have been discussing lately. Brooks and I have decided that it is time to move on; we have to see where things are at."

"What are you getting at Sean, you want to leave? Where will you go?" answered Brad.

"Brad, I fear we have been forgotten out here. We were thinking we could make our way to Bremmel; things should have died down by now. We should be able to gather supplies from there; then do our best to make it to Bagram down Route 76. It won't be easy, but I am confident we can make it. Bagram fell fast in the early days of the outbreak; maybe there is something left, maybe we can find an aircraft and get out of here.

"Oh yeah, and we want you to go with us."

Whiskey Tango Foxtrot
Tales of the Forgotten

By W. J. Lundy

Whiskey Tango Foxtrot
Tales of the Forgotten
© 2013 W. J. Lundy

This book is a work of fiction. The names, characters, places and incidents are products of the writer's imagination or have been used fictitiously and are not to be construed as real. Any resemblance to persons, living or dead, actual events, locales or organizations is entirely coincidental. All Rights Are Reserved. No part of this book may be used or reproduced in any manner whatsoever without written permission from the author.

PROLOGUE

It had been weeks since the first attack – since the day the world went dark and everyone had forgotten about them. The day he lost his company and most of his friends. They must have more to worry about than a half-dozen stranded soldiers in the back forty of the world. No contact, no messages, not even a flyover from a friendly aircraft. They were completely isolated and alone.

"Target, twelve o'clock. Primal on the wire," the spotter whispered.

Brad's team had done well for themselves, considering their situation. They had held up in the customs compound at Hairatan; they'd fortified it, made it a refuge. Their previous mission, in their old life, had been to patrol the streets looking for the Taliban. Now they worked with a former Taliban commander named Junayd, rescuing civilians and rebuilding in the furthest reaches of Afghanistan. Once enemies, they were now unified in a common goal to survive.

"Identified, primal on the wire," Brad whispered, pulling the rifle into his shoulder and letting his cheek rest on the butt stock. Gripping the heavy M24's handguards tightly, he forced himself to relax as he lined his dominant eye up with the scope.

The routines had become monotonous, the same tasks over and over. His deployment to Afghanistan had felt the same, but this was different. There was no real end to this, no day circled on a calendar to work towards. No goal to reach, no motivation to press forward. This was just surviving every day, day after day. They did patrols into the city to salvage goods and locate survivors. They had found plenty of the later, but never any soldiers. He feared his men might be the last remaining U.S. forces in country.

"Range twelve hundred meters, dial eighteen plus one click," ordered the spotter.

The compound was home now. Survivors of all types seeking refuge had come here looking for safety inside the fences. They all came together working the walls and doing the tasks that kept a camp running, soldiers and civilians side by side now. Brad's men knew the compound wouldn't stand against a large mass attack. How could it? Their own base had fallen in the first days, and it had been heavily fortified. That was when the attacks came in the thousands. More recently they would come at the walls in twos or threes. Unless something alerted them, it was very rare to see more than ten at a time during the daylight. No one wanted to think about a mob pressed against their gates, but they knew they were out there.

"Roger, eighteen plus one dialed in," Brad answered.

His men hated the patrols. But they were a necessary evil, essential to the survival of the group. This wasn't like hunting the Taliban, which could lead to days or even weeks of boredom, broken only by minutes of unrelenting violence. This was constant. The soldiers were almost guaranteed to run into conflict every time they left the wire. And unlike before, there would be no calls for medevacs or air support. During the last patrol Brad went on, they'd searched the village market. From all appearances, the place had been abandoned and well picked over, but they needed to break into the old storage warehouse to be sure.

"Wind from three o'clock, six miles per hour, dial wind right, two point three," came the spotter's adjustments.

The warehouse was infested with the primals. When they'd opened the large, double doors, they were immediately engaged. They often found hives of them behind locked, barricaded, and closed doors like this. In the early days of the attacks, families would seek refuge in their homes, securing themselves in, often with wounded loved ones in tow—not knowing that their injured family member would turn and attack them in their final hiding place. That was before they'd known how it spread, how deadly it was. Before they knew a deep cut or bite would bring on the rage.

"Roger, dialed two point three, target indexed," Brad whispered, making adjustments to the rifle without taking his eye off the target.

It had taken most of the day and a large amount of ammo to clear out that hive. They had no for sure strategy against them; the primals played by no rules. Primals massed quickly and would pour from every direction if they sensed prey. They had no fear of injury or death; they couldn't be suppressed; there was no shock and awe to use against them. Primals couldn't be intimidated into surrender.

Battle drills called for shutting down the immediate threat as quickly as possible, then getting very stealthy, running and hiding from the later waves of primals that always showed up. In the city it was pointless to attempt to stand your ground, there would always be too many. Stealth and escape were the only things that worked.

"Take the shot," the spotter whispered.

Who knew what they would do when the ammo ran out. Close combat with primals was a nightmare; they were fast and strong, and they never tired. They didn't hesitate to strike and they wouldn't quit if they thought a meal was nearby. Brad needed to make long term preparations, but his people were always too busy surviving to look to the future. They needed to make contact with the States, their families, and their command. They needed help.

"Firing," Brad said as he focused the sight picture and pulled the trigger during the natural pause in his breathing.

The SEAL Team Chief was the only one to have had contact with the military after the attacks, but even that was lost when the satellite phones batteries died. Sean told Brad that NATO had pulled out all of the soldiers in the first days. They had been re-called to defend their homelands. Brad's men were not so lucky, blindsided by the fog of war. The government gave little advanced warning that the attacks were coming; as always, *'the need to know'* didn't reach the soldiers on the ground or in remote camps. They were afraid if the intelligence about the biological attack leaked, the enemy would strike early, before the Special Forces could stop them. Either way they'd lost.

"Hit, head, target down," confirmed the spotter.

The fog of war and Murphy's Law had taken down innumerable members in the attacks. Now they were alone, lost and outnumbered. A dozen men from a lost patrol were of little concern to the big picture in the fight for humanity. The United States was under attack and fighting for survival. How could they spare resources to look for others when they were fighting for their own lives? Those were the arguments Brad used to justify the abandonment to his men, but he didn't have one for himself. As hard as it would be to leave the safety of this compound, the decision was clear. Someone needed to leave, to reach out; without support they wouldn't make it out here alone.

"Roger, hit," Brad replied, opening the bolt and chambering another round. This was his seventh kill this morning, and the start to a long watch.

1.

Forward Operating Base Bremmel

Zero day plus one.

He wasn't a bad soldier, just misunderstood. Sergeant Robert Logan was always in trouble, not on the job, but for things he did on his own time. His last adventure had caused him to oversleep and not show up on time for duty. That cost him his team leader position and sentenced him to a week of working in the chow hall. Now the rest of Echo Company was preparing for a patrol, and he was getting ready for a day slinging hash. Time in the mess hall sucks, but not as bad as watching your men roll out without you.

Robert was helping Corporal Méndez prepare his crew for today's mission; this would be his first as team leader. Robert was nervously quizzing him to make sure he was ready for the responsibility. Méndez told him to relax, that everything would be fine. He had a solid crew, Specialist Eric was a good driver, and Private Ryan was one of the best gunners in the company. Besides, it wasn't Robert's concern today, his job was serving up breakfast and the last thing he needed was to be late for work again. Robert shook his former teammates' hands and wished them luck on today's patrol, then walked away towards the chow hall.

It felt strange for Robert to be going to work without the body armor and weapons he was used to. He still carried his M9 pistol in a holster, but other than that he felt naked. Robert made his way to the mess hall and said good morning to the mess sergeant that ran the dining facility. She gave him a scowl, obviously not happy that she was always being assigned the other units' troublemakers to work in her facility. She needed the help though, and couldn't afford to turn anyone away.

She told Robert to get washed up and got him started on peeling and slicing hard boiled eggs. Robert was disgusted by the work assignment, but he settled in and got busy. Even though it sucked, he found the work surprisingly easy. He looked over the counter at the end of his work area and watched the soldiers begin to pile in for the morning meal service.

After a few minutes of peeling eggs, Robert decided to put himself on break and he wandered into the seating area. He saw a good friend of his and a fellow troublemaker, Staff Sergeant Bolder, just sitting down with his tray. Robert grabbed a cup of coffee and made his way over.

"Hey Bolder, how you doin', buddy?" Robert asked him as he sat down at the table across from his longtime friend.

"I'm good, I see they still got you on Kitchen Patrol, how long you got to do this for?" asked Bolder.

"Well, Sergeant Turner says I can be done at the end of the week if I stop being late all the time, but he said K.P. will be my permanent job if I screw up again. It's all bullshit, man. So anyway, what's new on camp?"

"Shit bro, didn't you hear? There was a big fight in the aid station last night … Yeah, from the medevac that brought in those wounded civilians yesterday," Bolder said.

"What? That was just a bunch of women and children and such. They were just cut up and scratched bad; I even helped unload them from the choppers."

"Yeah, that's the group," replied Bolder. "Seems they got into some shit, must have been on acid or something, 'cause a couple hours after the medics got them all patched up and into bed, them folks woke up angry as hell. They went ape shit on the medics. Damn, even the kids were biting and scratching at everyone. Had to pull security off the walls to handle them," explained Bolder.

"What the hell bro, that's crazy! So where they at now?" asked Robert.

"Oh, the Military Police got them all locked up, but man, it took half the guards on night shift to shut them down, wasn't cool, bro. I've never seen nothing like it. Anyhow, the captain gave all the guards the rest of the night off and told them to get some sleep. He called my crew in early to take over. They needed it though man, some of those guys had some deep scratches; a couple even got the shit bit out of them."

"Man, this place is crazy. They just need to send our asses home. Got drugged up civilians attacking us now; what's next, you know?" said Robert.

"I hear ya buddy, I hear ya," answered Bolder, shoveling in a forkful of eggs.

Robert was about to get up and head back into the kitchen when he heard a loud commotion coming from the main entrance. He turned to see what was going on just as two soldiers burst through the front door. One was dressed only in pants with no shirt; the other was wearing a T-shirt and shorts. The shirtless man had tackled a soldier in the doorway, and several others were trying to pull him off.

The mess sergeant ran from the kitchen looking angry as hell and ready to confront them. Yelling, she charged directly into the chaos. T-Shirt pushed off from the crowd and ran directly at her, grabbing at her shoulders. The mess sergeant screamed for help just as the crazed soldier took a snarling bite out of her exposed neck. Robert could see the man pull back with his mouth full of flesh, blood spurting out of the wound. The mess sergeant staggered backwards and fell to the floor.

Robert got over the initial shock of what he had just witnessed. He un-holstered his pistol, took aim, and pulled the trigger. He put two rounds into T-Shirt, knocking him back and away from the mess sergeant. Several soldiers ran to her and began first aid.

Robert stood dazed, with the smoking gun in his hands. To draw and fire had been instinctive, his training taking over; but now to see an American soldier dead by his hands stunned him. Robert holstered the weapon as the chaos woke him from his stupor. He ran over to help the other soldiers restrain the first shirtless man, but he was fighting hard and they were finding it impossible to pin him down.

With the mess hall in chaos, nobody noticed T-Shirt stumble and crawl back to his feet. He staggered forward with the two bleeding gunshot wounds in his chest and tackled a small female soldier providing aid to the mess sergeant. Robert heard her scream. Turning, he couldn't believe his eyes when he saw that T-Shirt was back up and attacking again. *What the fuck?* Robert thought. He started to rush towards the female to help against T-Shirt just as four more crazed soldiers ran into the crowd that had gathered outside the doors.

What the hell is going on? Robert again thought to himself. He stood and took a step backwards, fending off his feelings of panic. Off to the right he could see that the shirtless man was now winning the fight. He had taken a bite out of a soldier and a couple of others had nearly quit in exhaustion. To the left, T-Shirt had silenced the small female and was now wrestling with a third soldier. Back outside the doorway, it was a cluster of bloody bodies all battling for leverage. Fear had taken over and confusion was winning the fight.

Then the gunfire started outside. The first shots startled Robert, the familiar sounds again sparking his training; he redrew his pistol, putting two more rounds into T-Shirt and knocking him down for a final time. Stepping closer, he plugged a final round into his skull. Pivoting hard on his feet towards the shirtless man, he raised his weapon and emptied the magazine into his naked chest, ending the struggle. Shortly after he fired his last shot, the shirtless soldier stopped moving and slumped to the ground. The fight outside was growing, and one of the wounded soldiers jumped to secure the mess hall doors, locking out the madness just beyond them. A few more saw what he was doing and followed suit by piling tables and chairs against the entryway.

Robert turned to look around the room … the two attackers were down and dead. He saw at least four other soldiers lying on the floor bleeding heavily. Five others were in the room, most of them also covered in cuts and scratches. The cooks came from the kitchen into the dining facility to assist in giving first aid. He saw Bolder again; he had a long scratch down his arm from the fight with Shirtless, and Robert asked him if he was okay.

"Yeah I'm good. Man, that wasn't right. That's exactly what went down in the aid station last night. You think them civilians could have slipped these guys some of the same drugs?"

"I don't know Bolder, but those guys were tough as hell. I shot one twice and he still got up and kept fighting. What's going on outside? It sounds like a riot," answered Robert.

Robert and Bolder walked to a window and looked out. The camp was a mess; they could see soldiers fighting soldiers everywhere. Some had weapons drawn and were firing into masses of fighting men. Everyone was in a panic and in complete disorder.

"Bolder, we've got to get out of here. Let's get back to the company building and find out what's going on," Robert said.

With Robert leading the way, the two of them cut back through the kitchen and out a back door. The back of the mess hall was positioned against a long concrete T-wall that protected it from mortar and rocket fire. A service entrance led from the back of the kitchen and followed the wall around onto a dirt street. Robert made his way through the service area and guided Bolder onto the street. It suddenly grew quiet and the gunfire ceased. Only screams of agony and the voices of soldiers shouting orders remained in the air.

Robert rounded a corner and looked to the left. He saw that most of the fighting in front of the mess hall had stopped. There were a lot of bodies on the ground. Confused and shocked soldiers walked the camp, staring at the fallen. Robert and Bolder moved in the direction of the company buildings; they could see soldiers sitting on the ground with cuts on their arms and faces. Others were weeping and trying to provide aid to their friends.

Robert walked with Bolder across the open space. They stood stunned, looking at the destruction around them. There were two dead soldiers in front of them. The soldiers looked like they had been torn apart by animals. Another soldier lay to their left; he had a bandaged arm, and his chest and head showed fatal gunshot wounds.

"That's Erickson," Bolder said, pointing at the bandaged man. "He was one of the guards that got attacked last night."

The silence was suddenly shattered by sirens blaring and loudspeakers announcing, "*Incoming ground attack, all available personnel to assigned security sector.*"

"You got to be fucking kidding me! Let's go, Robert, time to get to work!" Bolder yelled before he turned and headed for the wall.

Robert looked at the pistol in his hand; he loaded his last magazine, then picked up a rifle off the ground next to a dead soldier and ran after Bolder towards the wall. They got to the front gate just in time to see a large jingle truck racing towards the entrance. The truck was going fast, driving erratically, and blaring its horn. The men on watch fired flares and warning shots but the truck raced on. When they were certain it wasn't going to stop, they opened up on it with their heavy machine guns. The large caliber rounds ripped into the engine block, skipping through the truck, blowing out the cab and killing the driver. The truck came to a rolling stop in a ditch just short of the first set of barriers.

A young officer with a gold subdued lieutenant's bar on his helmet pointed at Bolder and Robert. "You two! Get out there and secure that vehicle."

"Hooah sir," Bolder sarcastically grumbled back. He slapped Robert on the shoulder. "You ready for this, bro?"

"Lead the way," Robert answered.

They weaved through the barriers and slowly approached the truck. The destroyed engine made a clicking sound as it died and cooled off in the heat. The front was bleeding coolant onto the ground; steam and smoke billowed from holes in the hood. Robert rounded the front of the truck, sliced the corner with his rifle and aimed into the cab. He found a mess inside with little left to investigate.

They began to lower their weapons when they heard a whimper coming from the covered bed of the vehicle. Bolder gave Robert a quick hand signal and they pressed back to the rear of the jingle truck. Robert took a step back and raised his rifle, providing cover while Bolder lifted the canvas to peer inside.

"Oh shit," Bolder gasped.

Robert stepped forward to look inside and saw the bed of the truck was littered with wounded civilians, most of them children.

"Lieutenant! We need a medic up here!" Robert yelled back over his shoulder. The lieutenant and another young soldier ran forward to the truck and looked inside.

"Sir? You want me to call for a medic?" the young soldier asked.

"No, they're busy with the wounded inside, they won't have time for this shit!" the lieutenant snapped back in frustration.

They heard a soft voice from the front of the covered truck bed, quietly calling for help. Robert climbed over the tailgate of the truck and into the bed, moving forward until he found the man who spoke.

"I'm here," Robert said.

"Water," the man pleaded.

Robert yelled the request back at the men and the young soldier tossed him a small bottle of water. Robert opened the container and helped the man sip.

"Why did you run at our gate?" Robert asked. "Why didn't you stop?"

"We didn't run *at* your gate, we ran *to* your gate. We ran from *them*," answered the dying man.

"Ran? Ran from whom?" Robert asked.

The man gave Robert an exhausted, sad look. He raised his hand, pointing over and behind the men standing at the back of the truck. "From death," he said.

Robert strained to look into the distance. It was difficult to see from the darkness of the covered truck and out into the hot bright sunlight. Far off in the distance, through the waves of heat on the pavement, he could make out a large group of people headed in their direction. Robert looked back down at the man and saw that he had passed.

"Well shit, here it comes," grumbled the lieutenant, looking in the same direction. "Right on time; that would be the villagers from town coming to protest the dead civilians from last night. I'm sure this truck full of bodies isn't going to help things."

"L.T., the man in the truck said they were running away from that group; maybe it's more of what just happened inside. I don't think they're protestors," said Robert.

"Well, nice story, but he can't help us now. Let's get back to the barrier and get ready to meet our guests," the lieutenant argued.

Robert and Bolder turned, closed the tailgate, buttoned down the canvas cover on the truck, and then headed back to the camp's gate and barriers.

"I have a bad feeling about this, Bolder," Robert mumbled.

"I know, just stay sharp bro. I got your back," Bolder said.

They moved behind the barrier and took up a position just inside the open gate. Robert saw the mob moving closer. Yeah, they were definitely pissed off, they were even running! Robert had seen protests at Bremmel before, but usually they were pretty well orchestrated. This one appeared to be spontaneous, with no leader, and they were coming fast.

An Afghan soldier moved to the barrier and started yelling through a bullhorn, commanding the mob to stop approaching the base and to keep their distance. Several more Afghan soldiers dragged a heavy roll of coiled wire across the road, blocking the entrance to the barriers. But they kept coming. They passed a sign far out on the road that warned that violators would be shot if they approached the base. The mob continued to run.

The lieutenant ordered warning shots, and the machine gunner fired quickly over the crowd, but they didn't slow, didn't even flinch. "Gas!" the lieutenant shouted. The soldiers on the barrier fired tear gas canisters into the charging mob, but they never even paused. The CS grenades bounced off some of the protestors, knocking them to the ground, but they got back up and continued running. "Shotguns up!" the lieutenant yelled, panic growing in his voice. The Afghan soldiers raised shotguns and readied themselves for the mob.

The first wave hit the wire with a screeching roar, but that was quickly outdone by the sounds of the screaming crowd. Protestors were tangled and pushed deeper and deeper into the wire by those behind them. Eventually they collapsed and were pressed to the ground, their bodies covering the jagged strands of barbed wire. Screaming protestors from the back began to climb up and over the fallen, and resumed their charge at the base.

"Open fire!" the lieutenant screamed frantically as he stepped backwards. The first volley of shotgun rounds dropped a few of the charging protestors, but most of them made it to the barricades. The Afghan soldiers were firing as quickly as they could, but with little effect. They racked and fired into the crowd, quickly reloading as they expended every round. The rioters continued screaming and breaching the barriers, the shotguns seemingly worthless against them.

Robert quickly noticed why. They were firing crowd dispersal rounds and rubber bullets that bounced off the crowd or only temporarily slowed them. The lieutenant was expecting protestors, not a feral crowd of rioters. The mob started to push over the barriers. As the barricades tumbled, the mass of people flooded towards the gates. "Weapons free! Fire!" the now fully panicked lieutenant screamed.

Robert saw several of the Afghan soldiers drop their guns and turn to run; others just stood paralyzed by fear as the protestors breeched the barriers and swarmed over them. The M2 machine gun on the tower opened up into the crowd, knocking them down, but his angle was wrong. They were too close to the gates now, too close for him to stop them all. The rounds carved a path through the mob, but others continued to pour in and quickly filled the void as the gunner reloaded.

Robert and Bolder raised their rifles and fired almost point blank into the crazed mob. Robert thought his rifle wasn't working as he fired round after round into the charging protestors with no effect. A frenzied man broke free of the swarm and ran directly at Robert. Ignoring direct hits to the chest, he grabbed Robert in a bear hug. Robert tried desperately to push off but it was impossible with the weight of the crowd guiding the man into him. Robert tripped and fell backwards with the man on top of him. He struggled against the weight of the man and the stampeding of feet pounding into him. He felt the man in his face, could feel his breath against his scalp. All he could hear was the pounding footsteps of the crowd and the frenzied screaming of the mob.

Robert violently struggled with the man, trying to push him off or roll him to the side. The man pressed in tight to Robert's head and grabbed at his ear with his teeth. Robert screamed with pain and rage. He freed a hand and was able to draw his pistol, quickly pushing the barrel into the man's abdomen and firing four quick shots. Robert could feel the sticky warmth of the man's blood on his hands. The man bucked slightly, pausing only briefly before he continued to bite, gnawing deeper into Robert's forehead and face. Robert contorted his body, finally freeing the length of his arm. He painfully raised the pistol to the man's head and squeezed the trigger.

2.

Hairatan Customs Compound

Zero day plus thirty-two.

Brad sat on the roof of the warehouse looking out at the dark city. The fires had quit burning days ago; the blackness had blanketed the city. There was still an occasional scream, and sometimes a gunshot, but for the most part the city had grown silent over the past few weeks. The compound-turned-refugee-camp was growing in size. They had almost two hundred residents now. Most of them had come in the early days of the outbreak: hungry, scared and looking for a home.

Junayd's people would find them on their daily patrols, and if they were friendly, he brought them back to the compound. Brad didn't know how many had been turned away, if any. It was a conversation he didn't want to have. They left the questions of who to take in and who to turn away with the locals. Brad considered Junayd the mayor of this refuge; if anything, he thought of himself as the sheriff. The informal relationship had worked, and the camp was prospering, as well as any camp in a wasteland.

When Brad looked over the edge of the roof and into the compound, he could see his people moving about. *'His people', when did he start thinking of them as that?* Brad looked out at the gates and walls and saw soldiers patrolling the fences, standing watch alongside Junayd's men. The Afghan fighters didn't have the same training and discipline as his soldiers. Even so, they had proven themselves to be trusted warriors over the past month. Many times the Afghans had impressed him; they were very dedicated and loyal to the families they protected.

Brad descended the ladder back into the warehouse, walking through the living area and out into the cool night air. He found a quiet spot, and sat in front of the building that overlooked the gates and his men on watch. He was struggling with the offer that the SEALs had presented to him in recent days. They had asked him to leave this place, to attempt to make it back to Bremmel and beyond, back to society. It was becoming apparent that nobody was going to rescue them. *Were they really forgotten?*

Junayd's scouts had made several runs into some of the neighboring villages, but never returned with good news. They had once braved the bridge and attempted to visit the north. They found large packs of roaming primals. After several dangerous encounters, they wisely determined the risk was too great. The bridge was now completely barricaded; nothing would be able to pass it without a bulldozer.

Sometimes they would see the packs standing on the far side of the river. They probed and hunted for a way to cross. So far, the swiftly moving water had stopped them. Still, Brad worried what would happen when winter came. Would the primals freeze like the river? Or would they walk across the frozen waters?

Initially they had hoped the disease would run its course and the primals would succumb to it. That day never came. Even thirty days later, the numbers were just as great as before, and in fact were growing. It was true that they saw less of them during the daylight. Primals didn't like the heat.

On a cool, overcast day the killers were out in force. But when the sun was bright, you would only encounter them indoors, or occasionally in a shadow. At night they were the most dangerous. Primals would come out of their hiding places and hunt freely, roaming the streets and polluting the night air with their moans.

The damn moaning! It reminded Brad of the howling wolves and coyotes from his home in northern Michigan. The thought of home made him smile; it was a place far different from this. *I wonder if I'll ever see the green forest again?* he thought to himself. Quickly he put the idea away; it was dangerous to get distracted on the job. He shook his head, smiling again. *Am I even on the job anymore?*

The last one they'd killed was emaciated; its eyes were glazed over and the skin had pulled tight over its bones. Junayd's lead scout, Hasan, had found it tangled in the wire way out past the main fences on one of his patrols. The thing was obviously malnourished and beaten, but it still fought with the strength of five men. Hasan said even after he had removed its head, the primal's eyes had looked at him with hatred and rage until they went dark.

Hasan had proven to be a good hunter. Every day he took groups out to scout and salvage items from the city. Brad didn't know much about the man; he had been mostly silent and usually kept to himself. Even the other Afghans tended to keep their distance. Brad wondered what his story was. Junayd trusted him, and even Brad's own soldiers would volunteer to patrol with Hasan on occasion.

Brad rose to his feet and made his way into the guardhouse they had converted into their barracks. It wasn't the most ideal housing. It was drafty and dusty, and the cinder block walls and concrete floors were less than inviting. His men had done their best to make it cozy with items from the rail yard and things the soldiers had scavenged out on the daily patrols. His bunk was in a corner tucked back in the rear of the guardhouse. His area would be considered sparse at best. Brad had always been a professional soldier and had never taken the time to collect many things, but now there was even less. Next to his bunk he kept his personal possessions; nothing more than a large pack, his armor, and a rifle. He didn't own much now in this new life.

Brad sat on his bunk and looked around the room. Some of the soldiers were still up, but it wasn't like before in the barracks in Bremmel. There wasn't any horseplay, no playing of cards; the men had to keep quiet for fear of luring in the primals. No one was reading books; the guardhouse was too dimly lit at night for that. Laptops and game systems were a thing of the past. They now survived in a quiet solitude. Brad lay back on his rack watching the ceiling, wondering how things might be different at home, his real home. Maybe it *was* time to leave.

3.

Brad woke to the stench of the cooking Afghan slop and his stomach turned. If there was one thing they had plenty of, it was the cans of mystery meat. They had found nearly ten full train cars of the stuff. Nobody enjoyed it, but at least they wouldn't starve. He just couldn't get used to the taste and the greasy coating it left in one's mouth after eating it. Lately it was breakfast, lunch, and dinner. The soldiers had handed over most of the real food to the families, but occasionally they would have their meals augmented with rice and beans collected in the daily scavenge runs.

Brad sat up in his bed and grabbed his shower kit. Standing and stretching, he moved out to the communal showers they had built behind his new barracks. Miraculously they still had running water. Henry, his young driver with aspirations of being an engineer, said the water came from a well. The pumps were powered by solar cells that were installed on the roof. Brad really didn't care how all of it worked, as long as it did. He put the young soldier in charge of facilities, and he had done wonders in turning the place around. Henry's main pride and joy had been the solar water heater: water heated by the sun. It had made him a bit of a hero around camp.

Brad found Sean, the SEAL team chief, on his way to the showers. Sean was heavily bearded now, as most of them were.

"You have an answer for me on that offer yet?" Sean asked Brad with a smile.

"I do. I think you're right and I want in, but let me break it to Turner and the men first. I don't know how they will react," Brad answered.

"Fair enough Brad, but be quick about it, we plan to leave at first light tomorrow. We have a lot of preparations to make," replied Sean.

Sean left him alone and Brad continued on to the showers. They weren't much, just some piping shrouded with some heavy canvas. But it was enough, and he quickly found himself enjoying his solitude in the hot water. Even though they had all been warned to be brief in the showers, he took a couple of extra minutes today. He reluctantly exited the hot water, knowing it might be his last hot shower for a while. Brad gathered his things and returned to the barracks to ready himself for another long day.

After dressing in a clean uniform, Brad walked over to the soldiers' fire pit behind the guardhouse. He found a place on the large crate converted into a table and took a seat. One of the Afghans who worked the soldiers' kitchen nodded to him and brought him a steaming bowl of the slop, which Brad accepted with a forced smile. Turner, the unit's platoon sergeant, took notice of Brad and placed his own bowl in a wash basin, then walked over and took a seat next to him. Turner took a small tobacco box out of his jacket pocket, and laid it across his lap.

"So I was talking to Brooks this morning; he told me you were considering leaving with them," Turner said while fumbling with a scrap of paper and trying to roll a cigarette.

"Still messing with those cigarettes I see. You know you'll be out soon, and withdrawal is going to kick your ass," answered Brad.

"Nahh, I won't run out, the Afghan boys have been bringing me tons of this stuff, and one of them found a rail car topped off with it. I'll run out of paper before tobacco, and then I'll just switch to a pipe."

"Well, sounds like you have it all figured out then," chuckled Brad.

"So seriously, you really leaving us or what?" asked Turner, licking the cigarette then sparking a match to light it.

"Word sure travel fast here, I guess some things never change."

"So is that a yes then? The way you're jumping around the subject I'm assuming that it is." Turner took a long drag on his cigarette. "Hey man, seriously, don't worry about me, I got your back whatever you decide. I'm more concerned about the men, and they rely on you."

"I think it's for the best, Turner. We can't just sit here forever. I want to go see what's left down south, maybe we can contact the States from there, you know. And technically I am still on the job. I'm sure if they knew we were here, the Army wouldn't approve of us just getting cozy. It's time for me to move on." Brad rose to his feet. "I really do appreciate your support, Turner, I really do," he said as he walked past the basin and tossed in his bowl.

Brad made his way to the main gate. He spoke to the remainder of his men, informing them of his plan and that he would be leaving with the SEALs in the morning. Many volunteered to go with him; he explained they would be needed to provide security to the camp. Brad promised to return for them as soon as he could, and somehow he would make contact with the camp again. There were no arguments, and the soldiers shook his hand and promised to help him prepare his gear for the coming journey.

He went back into the guardhouse and took a seat on his bunk. Looking around his living space, he took stock of things he would need on the trip. He didn't have much that the Army didn't issue. Brad opened the mouth of his large rucksack and stuffed in his clothing and the remainder of his gear. He placed the most needed equipment on top or in the outside pockets. Tightly rolling his bedroll, he attached it to the top of his pack. He stared at his protective gas mask for a second before smiling and tossing it aside; it landed with a thud on the bulletproof plates that he had removed from his body armor long ago.

He checked and double-checked the ordnance on his vest. He still had twelve magazines for his M4 and three for his M9, plus a couple of frag grenades just in case. He looked over the snaps to make sure everything was securely fastened. He picked up the Sigma pistol, carefully removing the magazine and making sure it was topped off. For some reason he had started considering the pistol his good luck charm, even though he'd never fired it. Maybe the fact that he had never needed it made it lucky. Brad wiped the pistol off and tucked it into the smaller day pack that he had attached to the outside of his larger rucksack, then put on the overloaded vest and hoisted the heavy pack onto his back. Taking a last look around the room, he sighed, then headed out the door.

Brad found Brooks and Sean working on a late model Land Rover Defender in their makeshift motor pool situated between the warehouses.

"She was a gift from Junayd," said Brooks over his shoulder as he watched Brad make his way to them.

"You don't want to take the MRAP?" asked Brad.

"We thought about it, but decided it wouldn't be right. That MRAP makes a hell of a life boat if your men ever need to bug out of here in a hurry. I don't think I'd ever feel good about taking that piece of security away from them," explained Sean. "There won't be a lot of room, but we should do OK. Can you get your gear over here so we can start packing?"

Brad dropped the heavy rucksack and attached it to the vehicle's roof rack. He saw that the SEALs had done the same with their own bags. Unlike the SEALs, who carried an abundance of weapons, Brad still considered himself a light infantry man. He carried a standard issue 9mm pistol and his M4 carbine augmented with the suppressor he'd been given. On his vest, he carried a full combat load of ammunition and two M67 fragmentation grenades.

The SEALs, on the other hand, humped a much larger kit. Multiple fragmentation grenades and anti-personnel mines (claymores) were strapped to the outside of their packs. Both of them had suppressed long rifles attached to the tops of their rucksacks. Shorter MP5 submachine guns were always slung across their chest for quick access. They wore H&K MK23 pistols on their hips, and even smaller .22 caliber MKII pistols were carried in their packs. Brad thought it was overkill to carry so many weapons when you only had two hands, but he appreciated the firepower when it was needed.

They spent the rest of the afternoon taking inventory of food and ammo, and deciding what to bring. Water took priority for space, and then food. The team wouldn't have much more ammo than their personal allotment. There were large stores of it in the warehouse, but the team had unanimously decided that it would be better to leave it with the camp. There would be plenty of it at Bremmel, and they could always scrounge for more on the road. They finished off the packing with a row of four 5-gallon fuel cans strapped to a rack on the rear bumper of the vehicle.

"Ha! We look like damn hillbillies ready to move off to Beverly," said Brooks with a deep laugh.

The last night in camp was spent sitting on the roof of the warehouse with Junayd and his elders. Sean had his map laid out in front of them, and Junayd was marking it with the best sources of fresh water, and helping them to plan the safest route back towards Bremmel. Méndez came to visit Brad and gave him a bundle of letters his men had written to their families back home. Brad knew that Méndez had a large family and that the last month had been hard on him. He knew it was a pipe dream, but Brad promised that if there was a way, he would see that their letters got delivered. Méndez gave him a last thank you for everything he had done to help get them off the road; he shook his hand and left Brad alone.

Brad broke away from the group discussing the trip; he wandered off to a far corner of the roof and laid out his bedroll and blanket. He thought about what they were attempting to do, and tried to put the thoughts of the ambushed convoy and the visions of Bremmel out of his head. As hard as he tried to block it, the face of PFC Ryan and the night he'd died in the desert always played back in his head like a cheap movie. *I'm definitely going to need some counseling when I get home*, he thought to himself.

4.

Sean woke him just before dawn; he slowly brought himself to his feet and stretched out the aches that you get when you choose to sleep in a corner on a roof. Cole and Henry were on watch in the snipers' nest. Brad walked over to them and shook each of their hands and told them good bye. He walked back to the ladder well and lowered his way into the warehouse. Most of the occupants were still asleep, and he was careful not to wake them. He ventured out of the large overhead door that usually stayed open these days and headed towards the motor pool.

When he got there, he found Brooks making some finishing touches to the load on the vehicle. Brooks saw Brad and tossed him an energy drink.

"Sorry buddy, no coffee today but this has just as much kick," laughed Brooks.

Brad accepted the drink happily and helped him check the straps on the vehicle's roof rack. Sean walked over with a plate of foot bread sandwiches he had managed to scrounge up from the Afghan kitchen and handed them out. Taking a big bite from one, Sean paused to open the Defender's door, then jumped into the passenger seat. Taking that as a sign they were ready to leave, the rest of the team mounted up.

Brooks started the engine which purred to life; it was noticeably quieter than the MRAP. He put the Defender into gear and slowly moved towards the vehicle gate. When they arrived, they found a soldier on duty with one of Junayd's men. They both walked over to the Defender to greet them. Brooks put the truck in park, and Brad and Sean got out to shake their hands goodbye. Brad saw Hasan walk out of the guardhouse carrying a large green backpack and his AK47 slung over his shoulder.

"I would like to join you," Hasan said, dropping his pack next to the already overloaded vehicle.

"I don't know, Hasan. Nothing personal buddy, but this truck is already bursting at the seams, and another mouth to feed splits our food supply even more," said Sean.

"That is true, friend, but I also know the area. I know the tribes. I can be useful in finding more food. I will not be a burden to you, and four guns in the fight is better than three," Hasan answered. Sean looked over at Brooks, who gave nothing more than a shrug of his shoulders.

"What do you think, Brad?" Sean asked.

"It's his country, who am I to tell him no? The more the merrier, right?" Brad answered with a grin.

"Okay then, throw your bag on the roof and get in," Sean said to Hasan, smiling.

They made their way down the city streets. Occasionally, the vehicle would pass a building and they would see a primal move out of a darkened alley or a doorway to moan at them. The sun was just beginning to break the horizon and the temperatures were cool, so they knew the primals would be active until at least mid-day. They were willing to takes those chances and decided it would be an acceptable risk, especially since they were mobile and moving at a high rate of speed. Brooks made a few passes down side streets and one extra unnecessary turn down a long road before cutting onto the Hairatan road. They hoped the extra maneuvering would make it harder for the primals to follow them out of the city.

There is only one way in or out of the city located on the northern border of Afghanistan—and that is the Hairatan road. The other path to civilization would have been through Uzbekistan to the north and over the river. With the bridge out and the packs roaming the other side of the river, the Hairatan road was their only option. Brooks followed the road carefully, easing the Defender onto the cleared lane of the highway that Brad and his soldiers had opened up almost a month earlier when they'd first entered the city.

As the team made its way down the highway, Brad recognized the dead bus blocking the far lane when they passed it; he also knew that the other MRAP rested silently in a ditch on the other side. Slowly the congestion of twisted and broken vehicles thinned out and the road started to clear. Brooks found a comfortable spot near the center line of the highway and eased the vehicle into a cruising speed of forty miles per hour.

They drove for hours. Brad watched Brooks drive with a look of confidence as he avoided obstacles. Brooks wasn't an easy man to get to know; he wasn't a social creature like Sean. In the past, it was common for soldiers to ask others questions about home, families, or where they were from. More recently, it was considered taboo to talk about such things. Many soldiers like Brooks would consume themselves with work to avoid personal feelings. Brooks was all business, typically only showing his face when there was a job to be done. The big man even spent his down time preparing for his up time. Brad rarely saw him joke or slack off with the rest of the men. Today Brooks was on the clock and held the wheel firmly, clearly aware that it was his responsibility to keep them safe.

Brad began to space out watching Brooks; the hot sun and the lulling sounds of the tires humming on the pavement caused his eyelids to become heavy. He caught himself nodding off more than once, often waking with a start. The Defender purred down the road, and the non-descript countryside going by in a blur made it hard to stay awake. They curved around and away from the river before entering the vast open terrain. Brad looked out and saw nothing but open dunes; the green was fading into the red and tan shades of the desert as he rested his head against the window and drifted off to sleep.

He woke to the sounds of crunching gravel and lifted his head. They had pulled off the road and Brooks was easing the vehicle up to a walled-in villa. It looked to be a large, two-story house surrounded by an eight-foot wall. From the condition of the place, it looked to have been abandoned long before the outbreak, but you could never be sure in Afghanistan. Brooks parked the Defender where it could not easily be seen from the road and killed the engine. The men got out, stretched, and checked their weapons.

"This is the place. Junayd said it would be empty and easy to defend," Sean declared, walking towards the wall's gate. "Brad, you want to help me clear the house?"

"Okay, right behind you," Brad replied as he grabbed his M4 and screwed the suppressor onto the barrel.

Sean walked over to the heavy wooden doors that marked the entrance to the courtyard; he had his silenced MP5 at the ready and waited for Brad to join him.

"What do you make of this?" Sean asked, pointing. The heavy wooden door was covered with scratches; some of the gouges looked to be stained with blood. Sean pointed at a crack in the door where Brad saw what looked to be a broken finger nail still stuck in the groove.

"What the hell? Someone wanted in here pretty damn bad," answered Brad.

He took a step back away from the door and raised his rifle while Sean pulled on the handle. The door didn't budge and was clearly locked from the inside.

"Hmm, we seem to have found ourselves in a bit of a pickle," Sean mused.

"Well it's obvious nobody is home, maybe we should just continue on our way down the road," chimed in Brad.

"Nope. Sorry buddy, this is our stop. I want to hit Bremmel in daylight tomorrow; that means we stop here for tonight."

Brooks walked over with a large crow bar and tried to stick it into the door to pry it open. The door had a steel frame and lip that made it hard to set the bar. He tried to get it into a good position, but any amount of force would just pop it out. Finally giving in to frustration, Brooks pulled the Defender up close to the wall.

Brad, shaking his head, said "Screw it," and climbed up onto the hood of the vehicle, then high onto its roof. He turned to look at the wall, checking to make sure the top wasn't covered with broken glass or nails, which was common in this area to deter thieves. Satisfied that the way was safe, he grabbed hold of it and pulled himself on top.

He could see down into the courtyard and at the lonely two-story home. The entire house was circled by the wall; the building was horseshoe-shaped and its mouth opened towards the wall's entrance. Brad looked left and right several times; although his instincts were tingling, he eased himself flat on the wall. Seeing nothing, he grabbed on tightly and swung his feet over the edge. Hanging by his fingers, he let go and dropped the last couple feet to the ground, landing with a thud. Brad called over the wall to say that he was in, and then moved back to the door.

He readied his weapon and took another look all the way around to make sure he was alone, then examined the door and found it was locked in place by a large steel bolt. Through one end of the bolt was an antique-looking padlock that prevented Brad from turning and sliding the bolt. He called back over the wall to tell the men what he had found.

"Stand back!" Sean yelled. "I'm going to toss over the crowbar."

Brad took a step to the side, then saw the crowbar sail over the door and hit the cobblestone with a loud metallic *CLANG* which echoed off the building's walls.

After picking up the crowbar, he went back to the wall and placed the flat end of the bar against the bolt in the door. As he started to apply downward pressure, he heard a distant rattle inside the house, as if furniture had just been knocked over. Brad froze in place and turned to look at the house. He waited and listened but, hearing nothing, continued to pull on the bar. Suddenly there was a loud crash, and more sounds of tumbling furniture coming from the house behind him. He spun around to look at the front door, located at the bottom of the horseshoe, and was shocked when he saw it rattle from a booming impact.

"Ahh, Sean? I think I have a problem," he called out.

"I'm assuming that isn't you making all of that noise in there?" Sean called back over the wall.

"That would be a correct assumption," Brad yelled back. He applied more pressure to the bar and, disappointed, did not even feel the bolt budge. He heard another loud *BOOM* against the front door. Brad pulled the bar from the bolt and tried to ease it into the door frame. He pulled as hard as he could and the door itself began to split, but it was still solidly sealed shut.

Brad heard another thundering *BOOM*, and glanced back just in time to see the front door of the house start to give. He dropped the crowbar and turned to face the door; taking a knee, he brought his rifle up and tried to adjust his eyes on the doorway nearly twenty feet away. He watched the door shake again from an impact, freeing dust from the boards and the overhang. Brad pulled the rifle tight into his shoulder, aimed where he hoped a head might be on the other side of the door, and squeezed the trigger. Three rounds, one after another, poked holes into the wood. There was a momentary pause in the pounding on the door, then a thud. Brad let out a sigh of relief just as another loud *BOOM* sounded out. Brad lifted his rifle back to his shoulder and fired another three rounds into the door. Another crash, and this time the door gave way.

The door flew open and a primal dressed in white and covered with gore tumbled forward. Not expecting the door to give, its momentum took it to the ground. Brad lowered his point of aim and pumped aimed shots into the thing's head. He blinked his eyes, trying to get them back into focus on the dark doorway, just as he watched five more pouring out. They were coming at a full sprint. Brad took out the leader with quick shots to the head, then watched it slump to the ground, tripping up a female behind it. He kept firing on the others as they closed the distance. He clipped one in the top of the forehead, making it fall. "Two left," he murmured to himself as he pivoted and shot one in the face.

The last one collided with him in a hard impact that forced him back against the door. Brad dropped his shoulders and pushed the rifle between them as hard as he could to break the primal's grip. He knocked it down and at the same time he fell backwards onto the ground. Still on his back, he propped up on an elbow and tried to raise the rifle. In his peripheral he could see two more stepping out of the house, and the one that had tripped earlier was getting to its feet.

Directly in front of him, he could see that his current play date was rolling back to its belly and pushing itself up. "Fuck me," Brad said to himself, dropping the rifle and drawing his M9. He quickly pulled the trigger, punching three holes into his date's neck and face, killing it. He rolled to his side just as the other three closed on him. Before he could take aim, Brad heard the rapid firing of Brooks' MP5 as rounds ripped into the charging primals. Brad watched as their heads exploded and their bodies collapsed to the ground. He stared at the fallen, motionless primals in the dirt, then dropped to his back in complete exhaustion.

Brooks lowered himself off the wall, stepped over Brad and walked toward the heavy door. He looked at the antique lock and held it in his hand. Letting go of the lock he let out a grunt, took a step back and fired a shot into the lock, shattering it. He fidgeted with the lock, freed it from the bolt, then pulled the bolt and swung the door open. Sean and Hasan stepped inside.

"Wow, you should have just opened the door and let us help," gasped Hasan as he looked at all of the primal bodies lying in the courtyard.

"You OK buddy?" asked Sean, extending his hand to Brad.

"I'm fine, but next time somebody else goes over the wall first," Brad said, taking Sean's hand and being pulled to his feet.

The team got themselves together and slowly approached the open door. All of the first floor windows of the villa had been boarded shut, and the windows on the second floor had the drapes tightly closed. They inspected the bodies on the ground and found them to look the same as the ones recently found in Hairatan: emaciated, with skin taut over their bones. The team stepped past them and stacked up on the door.

"Probably not much in there after all the noise Brad made, but you can never be too careful," Sean said. "Brad, you go right with me, Brooks, take Hasan to the left." The men gave thumbs up, and Sean turned on the light attached to his MP5. The rest of the team followed suit and they entered the dark doorway.

Brad followed Sean into a large empty foyer, while behind him Brooks and Hasan entered and cut to the left and moved out of sight. Sean moved quickly and efficiently swept the room, then waited beside a door for Brad before he entered the next. Forcefully swinging open doors, they swept into rooms checking all of the corners. They continued like this until they met Brooks and Hasan back at the main entrance.

With the full team once again joined, they formed back into a line. The stairs leading to the second story were offset into a wall at the back of the foyer. Sean gave a hand signal and the men stacked up at the base of the stairs and began their ascent toward the top. When they reached the open space at the head of the stairs they fanned out, each man covering a sector.

The team entered a large, sparsely furnished sitting room. What furniture there was had been tossed randomly around the space. Sean walked to an outer wall and ripped down a set of the heavy drapes covering a window, letting sunlight flood in and over the floor. There were bloody bandages and rags piled in a corner, and what looked to be empty food containers and dishes in another. "The things Brad killed in the courtyard must have sought shelter here when still human," mumbled Hasan.

"Yeah, probably wounded; they barricaded themselves seeking refuge from whatever was outside the gate while they slowly turned themselves," Brad answered back.

They said little while they walked back downstairs. Brad and Hasan dragged the primals' bodies to a far corner of the courtyard. They opened the heavy wooden door as wide as it would go and backed the Defender into the safety of the walls, closing the door behind them and locking the bolt.

They found very little else of use in the home. Upstairs, Hasan found a worn Enfield rifle and a bandoleer of ammo to match. He propped it carefully inside the entry door to the house, deciding he didn't need it and would leave it for a future visitor. None of the team had any interest in sleeping in the house, so they spread their bedrolls in the courtyard and, using dried wood, built a smokeless fire just large enough to heat their dinner. Brad volunteered to take the first watch. He climbed atop the Defender and settled into a comfortable position where he could see over the wall.

5.

As the sun gradually dropped below the horizon, the temperature began to drop with it. Darkness came quickly and was accompanied by the howling of the primals. Brad was disappointed to hear them; he had hoped they would be things of the city and wouldn't venture out into the desert as much. Junayd's men had rarely reported seeing them in the desert sands during the heat of the day. The scouts had always returned to the compound before sundown, never spending a night outside the protection of the walls. As it grew darker and the air cooled, the howling grew louder. Brad heard the stirring of the men on the ground and soon he found Sean sitting beside him on top of the vehicle.

Sean had his night vision spotting scope in his hand and was scanning the horizon. Brad watched him search, then stop to focus intently on some far off object.

"Now what is this?" Sean whispered. Brad observed Sean's face contort in concentration as he scanned. "Well I hadn't expected this," he whispered again, handing the scope off to Brad.

Brad put the scope to his eye but saw nothing other than the greenish hue of the desert sands. Sean lifted his hand, grabbed the scope, and guided Brad's eye to a spot about three hundred meters into the distance.

"Oh," Brad said. Looking through the scope, he saw a group of fifty to a hundred primals. They were back deep in a berm of sand. Most of them stood and walked in a circle with their noses to the wind, howling that scream, that deep moan. Brad watched as others would rise up out of the sand and get to their feet. After a pack was formed, they broke up into groups of ten to twelve and wandered off into the desert.

"What are they doing?" Brad asked.

"Looks like hunting parties. They must sleep or hibernate during the day, only to awaken and hunt for prey at night," said Sean. "I've seen lions do the same thing in Africa."

"No way, Sean. You think these things are like lions?" Brad asked.

"Keep your voice down. I'm just saying, I saw those things dig out of the sand. Something in them must tell them to stay out of the sun all day. Then they wake up at night. I don't know what to make of it, but in Africa I've seen lions do the same thing. They lay low all day, then hunt in packs under the cover of darkness," Sean answered back. "Doesn't matter Brad, this doesn't change anything. We'll still seek shelter at night and only move during the day." Sean glanced at him. "You look spent Brad, why don't you try and grab some sleep? I'll take the rest of your watch."

Brad lowered himself off the Defender and leaned against the back of it. His head was filled with so many things he couldn't think straight. *I need a drink,* he thought to himself. Frustrated, since he knew that wasn't going to be possible for a while, Brad made his way back to his pack and bedroll. He couldn't help but look at the doorway to the house from which the primals had rushed out and attacked him. He sat his pack against the side of the house and rested against it, pulling his blanket over himself. He laid his rifle across his lap and put the now familiar Sigma pistol at his side. "Tonight won't be a night for sweet dreams," he said to himself, and then drifted to sleep.

He was abruptly awakened with a hand across his mouth and Brooks' face close to his. Brooks held a finger over his lips and slowly released the hand from his face. Brad closed his eyes tightly and opened them slowly to try and wake up. He looked around and saw that everyone was gathered in the sleeping area. Brad looked to the top of the Defender and wondered why no one was on watch. It didn't take long to get an answer to his question. From outside the heavy wooden door he heard a thump, then scratching against the wood. Brad sat like a stone, watching the faces of Brooks and Sean who calmly held their rifles in their laps, intently focused on the wall's door. Hasan was sitting stoically farther to the back with his AK in his hands.

They spent the night watching the door and each other, sometimes having to shake a boot if one of them nodded off and began to snore. The scratching continued until the very early hours of the morning and quit just as the sun was beginning to come up.

Brooks stood and crept to the front of the Defender and slowly lifted his body onto the hood, then stood to look over the wall. Standing for a long time, he finally jumped down and gave the all clear.

"You know, Sean, I'm really starting to second guess myself for coming on this expedition; it didn't say shit about lions in the brochure," Brad quipped.

"Oh, you know you were bored chilling in that compound. You're very welcome for the rescue and you can put the charge for excitement on my tab," Sean snapped back quickly. "Hey guys, what do you say we hit a drive-thru for breakfast today. I'm kind of in a hurry to put some distance on this place. I wasn't getting the whole welcome guest vibe last night." Sean threw his bag on the top of the vehicle.

The team nodded in agreement before Hasan asked, "what is a drive through?" causing laughs all around.

With the bags stowed safely on the roof rack, they boarded the Defender. Brad opened the heavy door and Brooks eased the vehicle out through the doorway and stopped in front of the walls. Brad closed the door and stared at the bolt. In the end he decided to leave the door unlocked and just dropped the latch to keep it from swinging open. Who knew when someone else might seek the safety of these walls and Hasan's gift of the Enfield rifle? Brad walked back to the rear seat and piled into the Defender. As they rolled out, they all looked at the dune in the distance and wondered if there were a hundred sleeping primals under the sand.

6.

The Defender continued its journey down the Hairatan road. The farther they got from the city, the less vehicles they saw on the sides of the abandoned highway. The road opened up and Brooks was more comfortable driving faster. They rode in silence; occasionally one of them would point out in the distance a primal standing in the shadows of a rock, or a suspicious figure near a mud-walled dwelling. On a mission to make it to Bremmel before dusk, they did not stop to investigate.

It was nearly noon when they came on the abandoned MRAP in the center of the road. Brad told the team how Sergeant Turner had been forced to abandon it once it ran out of fuel. Brooks pulled close to it and stopped. Sean wanted to give it a quick once over to make sure there was nothing of value left inside.

They stepped out of the Defender. Sean and Brad moved towards the MRAP while Brooks and Hasan headed to the shoulder to relieve their bladders. "Like I said, Sean, they took everything from it, there's nothing left," Brad said as they walked around the stripped-down vehicle. When they got to the back, Sean reached up and opened the large door to the crew compartment and looked inside.

"Hmm, was it like this when you left it Brad?" Sean queried.

Sean stepped aside and allowed Brad to stand on the step and look into the vehicle. The inside was covered with blankets. Some of the seats had been removed; there were cans of food on the shelves and a water bladder made from some kind of animal skin hanging from the ceiling. It was obvious the space had been recently occupied.

"What the hell? Someone is living in here," Brad said.

"Yeah, but who?" asked Sean as he carefully scanned the surrounding desert. "And where are they now?"

They searched the area all around the MRAP for tracks but found no other signs of the occupants. There were plenty of cans of food in the MRAP and the water bottle was more than half full. There were no signs of weapons, or any clue as to how many were hiding here.

"What do you think, Sean?" Brad asked.

"I don't know, but we can't hang out. Let's leave this as we found it," Sean said.

"What about the people? We can't leave them," Brad said.

"Maybe they heard us coming and are watching from the desert. Worse case they got eaten by lions last night, either way it's not our mission," said Sean.

"Damn, always the optimist, aren't ya?" Brooks chimed in.

"Let's leave them a note directing them to the compound; these people deserve a chance," offered Hasan.

"It's a risk. We don't know who they are, but I guess if they are too weak to fight our team of four, they wouldn't do much against the compound," Sean said.

Hasan wrote a note in multiple languages and drew a map. The map showed the location of the walled villa on the road, and then directed them into Hairatan. He was careful not to lead them to the compound but instead to a place in the city where he knew Junayd's fighters would find them on their daily patrols. Hasan placed the note on the center of the makeshift bed inside the MRAP and closed the door. "I guess this is the most we can offer," Hasan said.

They boarded the Defender, feeling as if too much time had already been spent here. Pulling back onto the road, Brooks sped up and they lost sight of the MRAP behind them. Brad wondered who they had been, and felt pangs of guilt for not doing more for the mysterious people.

They would make good time now; the road was clear and even the potholes were farther apart. Brad sat his back in his seat and watched the scenery quickly go by. Soon they made it to the dead end 'T' intersection where the Hairatan road disappeared into the desert. A sign told them they were entering Route A76 and offered them the choices of west towards Mazar-e-Sharif and Bremmel, or east. Brooks slowed the vehicle, looking both ways out of habit, and turned the Land Rover west towards the Forward Operating Base.

Brad started thinking about the last time he'd been at the base, and hoped it had all been a bad dream, or something he'd imagined. Maybe they would pull up to the gates and find that Task Force Raider had survived. He would see his friends working the walls, happy to see him. He was dreaming of a warm reception; maybe he'd be able to sleep in his own bed tonight.

7.

His fantasies were quickly crushed when they rounded the bend and found the lonely Forward Operating Base. Brooks pulled the vehicle into cover just shy of a mile from the gates. They exited the Defender and observed the FOB cautiously through their binoculars. Just as Brad had seen it last, the base was a mess. The front gate was hanging open and, from their high angle, they could see that most of the tents had been knocked down or badly damaged. They spotted no sign of movement, but they were still wary and decided to tactically approach Bremmel. They left the Land Rover hidden where Brooks had parked it and prepared to move in on foot.

Each man carried a large empty duffle bag on his back as they slowly walked in a column down the approach to Bremmel. Brooks walked point while the rest of them followed. When they got closer to the gate, they began to smell the telltale stench of death. Near the first set of concrete barriers that stood in front of the base was a large truck in the ditch. Brooks put up his fist to signal the rest to halt as he approached the rear of the large vehicle. He lifted the canvas flap covering the truck and, after a quick look inside, shook his head, signaling the truck was clear, and they walked past it.

The team moved slowly to the barrier and saw bodies strewn around it, torn apart by heavy weapons fire. There was a tangle of corpses forced through, and into, the camp's barbed wire barriers. Brooks paused to remove his wire cutters, and, while Sean held the wire steady, he cut a path through it. They moved past the wire to the first set of concrete barriers. Shotguns lay on the ground with spent shell casings nearby. Sean stopped to pick up a spent shell and looked at it. "Rubber bullets, poor bastards," he said while tossing the shell back to the ground. Hasan reached down to retrieve one of the Mossberg shotguns.

"Don't bother, Hasan, we don't have the ammo for them," Brooks said.

They moved further in toward the gates, cautious not to step on the rotting bodies. Brad paused to tie his shemagh over his face; the smell was beginning to get to him, and he felt the urge to vomit. Brad looked up and saw the silent barrel of a machine gun poking out from the guard tower, the gunner long dead. Bodies of those in uniform were now mixed with the dead civilians. They moved to the gates and saw another large cluster of the fallen.

Looking at the spot where the camp's security must have made their last stand, Sean turned and faced his men. Looking at Brad and Hasan, he asked, "Are you two OK to continue inside? Brooks and I can do this alone."

"No, I'm okay. I have your back, let's just keep going," answered Brad.

Hasan nodded and pulled his rifle into his shoulder, obviously afraid.

"Okay then, let's keep it tight. If we have problems, we bound back to the gate and haul ass for the Land Rover," instructed Sean. The team once again fell in line behind Brooks, who slowly walked through the gates. Brad could see many scattered bodies around the grounds of the camp.

Just inside the gate, a 9mm pistol sat on the ground next to a pair of badly trampled bodies. Hasan reached down, grabbed the weapon, and dropped it into his duffle bag. Then they walked on down the gravel road that led through the center of the camp. The only sound was that of the wind beating the torn tent fabric. Brooks led them to a point near a concrete bunker and took a knee.

The team huddled together and Sean asked Brad where the communications shack was located. Getting a working battery and charger for the satellite phone was a priority; after that, it would be food and ammo. Brad pointed to a building up the road, and Brooks once again stepped off first to lead the way. When they got to the building, Brooks held up his fist again. He pulled his silenced pistol and looked to Sean who did the same.

"You two stay out here and watch our backs. If you see anything, don't call out, just tap on the door. Okay?" Sean said to Brad and Hasan.

Brad nodded and took a knee in a location where he could see all approaches to the building. Hasan did the same on the opposite side of the door. Brad watched as Sean and Brooks opened the door and disappeared into the room, feeling guilt at his joy that Sean hadn't asked him to help clear the building.

Brad heard the footsteps of the SEALs fade as they walked deeper into the communications shack. He jumped when he heard two muffled gunshots come from inside, followed by two more. Brad was growing anxious and was debating whether or not he should go in and check on the SEALs when the door slowly opened and his friends walked out of the building.

Sean came out first with Brooks following; they walked forward and took a knee on the road next to Brad. Sean looked at Brad and shook his head. "No good on the batteries. That place has been torn apart. Where is the supply building located?"

Brad looked down the street and pointed to a large, steel-sided pole barn. "That's brigade supply; anything we need, we should be able to find in there."

They got back to their feet and followed Brooks down the road.

Brooks raised his fist again and they all took a knee. Brooks pointed ahead and he showed two fingers. Puzzled, Brad looked in the direction he had pointed but didn't see anything. He slowly moved forward to Sean. Sean pointed his rifle in the direction and Brad looked down the barrel. Off in the shadows of the blast wall, two uniformed figures were standing as still as statues staring back at the wall. Brad lifted his own rifle and through his advanced optics he could see they were primals, but they weren't moving; they just stood as if meditating.

Sean signaled for Brad and Hasan to stay put as he and Brooks moved forward. Brad watched the two men silently slip ahead. When they were within ten feet of the primal they let their rifles hang from their tactical slings and drew their knives. Taking the last few steps, they dropped into fighter's stances and stabbed the primals through the backs of the head in perfect timing. They caught the bodies, slowly lowered them to the ground, and made their way back to the team. Brooks gave them a thumbs up and continued toward the supply building.

The supply warehouse sat at the end of the street where it dead ended— right at a large set of sliding doors that could be opened for trucks making deliveries. In the center of the sliding doors was a smaller steel entry door that currently was hanging open. The team moved slowly to the open entrance. Just feet from the door they all took a knee. Sean gave the signal for them to stack up and they quietly entered the open warehouse.

Once inside, Sean stopped and turned back to quietly close the door; he then turned the bolt to lock it behind them. "I don't want nothing sneaking up on us while we're shopping," Sean whispered.

The supply building was really more of a large garage that had been subdivided by cages. The cages were filled with shelves and stocked heavily with supplies. They were hit with the smell of stinking bodies and human waste that always accompanied primals. The room was nearly blacked out, but Sean shook his head at Brad when he went for his flashlight. Instead, they pulled on their night vision goggles. Brad suddenly felt bad for Hasan, who was behind him and blind in the darkness. He grabbed the man's hand and indicated for him to hold on to the back of his jacket. Brad made a mental note to find Hasan some goggles of his own.

They crept into the warehouse, stopping frequently to listen. When they reached the first cage door, Brooks went to open it and found it latched from the inside. He let his rifle hang from its sling and gingerly reached far inside the cage. Stretching for the latch and twisting hard, he was just able to reach it. He tugged at the latch and heard the click as it unlocked, then pulled his arm back through the cage and opened the door. They all cringed when it gave a loud screech as it swung open.

They froze in place and listened. After a moment there was a thump in the back of the cages and a primal came walking from around a large set of shelves. It was blinded in the blacked out room, and several times it bumped into the walls making more noise. Brad watched it in the green glow of his goggles. It was sniffing the air trying to find its prey, but the hunt didn't last long. Once it got close enough for Sean to have a confident shot with his suppressed MK23, he killed it with a single round to the head. The thing teetered for a second then fell to the floor.

They listened quietly. Brad hoped that the others couldn't hear his heartbeat, and wondered how much worse it must be for Hasan with no night vision at all. They heard another tumble of objects and a second primal staggered around the corner. Sean waited and watched as it walked towards the first. Sean took another shot, dropping it to the ground. Before Brad could let out a sigh of relief, a third primal rounded the corner. This one was moving faster and tripped over the second downed primal before Sean could pull the trigger. The primal moaned when it hit the ground and twisted hard, trying to rise. Sean had to fire twice to connect with it. There then came a louder crash of boxes and objects from behind the shelves.

"I think things are about to get difficult," Brooks whispered as he signaled for them to back up, closing the cage door and pulling on it until he heard the click of the latch resetting. Brooks took another step back until he was online with Sean, then both of them holstered their suppressed MK23s, lifted their suppressed MP5s, and turned on the weapons lasers. Invisible to the naked eye, Brad saw the IR beam illuminate from the front of the submachine guns through his night vision goggles.

There was another loud clattering of objects from behind the shelves, then the loud moan the primals used to announce the hunt. At first they came around the corner two at a time, then they seemed to all rush at once, fighting each other for a chance to be first to get at the men. As quickly as they came, the SEALs lined them up with the beam and with quick pulls of the trigger sent the primals tumbling to the ground. Soon there was a pile of bodies at the corner, and the others were falling and tripping trying to get to the team. Sean and Brooks made easy work of putting them all down. As suddenly as it had started, it was over, and again the supply building was quiet; at least *was*, until the pounding started at the door behind them.

First it was a thud against the steel door, then another thud followed by the pounding, and finally, the frenzied banging and snarling that let the men know a mob had gathered outside. Brad turned to look and saw to his relief that the door was well built and holding. He looked to the right just as the thunderous pounding started to resonate from the large sliding cargo doors. They were rattling hard but were also holding. Brooks rose to his feet and walked to the doors to ensure they were bolted and tightly secured. He pulled out plastic chemical light sticks and began snapping and shaking them until they glowed a fluorescent yellow, then tossed them around the room. Hasan, relieved by the illumination, relaxed his grip on Brad's back and stood upright.

"What do we do now?" Hasan asked.

"Well, looks like we have gotten ourselves into a bit of a predicament. Brooks, can you get to some high ground and see what we are dealing with outside? I'll take these guys through the cage and verify it's clear," Sean said.

"On it, Chief." Brooks dropped his pack and made for a narrow ladder that led high into some storage spaces in the rafters. Sean looked back and spoke to Brad and Hasan, who were still standing in disbelief, looking like scared children.

"You two ready for this? Let's move through this mess."

"I'm ready," Brad whispered back, his voice barely audible over the pounding and moaning outside.

Sean reached through the cage door and undid the latch. He turned on the flashlight attached to his MP5 and Brad did the same, lighting the way. They now could clearly see the mess that was in front of them. Ten to twelve primal bodies lay twisted and contorted at the end of the narrow walkway and the corner to the storage area. Sean quietly walked past them, being careful to keep his feet far away from the pile, ever cautious that one might only be unconscious.

They wound around the pile and turned the corner into the shelving area. The stench of body odor and human waste hit them hard. They all pulled out scarves and wrapped them tightly around their faces. Creeping down the narrow aisle, they made their way to a void in the storage area where they found tattered cardboard, clothing, and human hair.

"Looks like we found us a primal nest," whispered Sean. "This must be where they went to sleep during the day. The warehouse door was open … so there must be another way into this cage."

The area was a mess and covered with feces. "Careful not to get any of that on you, it may be contaminated," Sean called out as they made their way through the void.

Entering the storage shelves, Sean slung his rifle and reached onto a shelf to turn on a battery-powered lantern, illuminating the space with a soft white light.

"There," Brad said, pointing at a locked cabinet marked '*Sensitive Items*'.

Sean looked at the locked door and pulled out a small jimmy bar he carried in his gear. Slamming the bar into the door, he pulled hard and the door flew open.

"Jackpot!" he said, pointing to a stack of boxes of brand new satellite phones. "These are the same model as ours; even if they aren't active we can use the batteries. Hopefully we can power ours up." Sean ripped a box open and stuffed the phone and accessories into his pack; he then opened two more boxes to grab just the batteries out of them. He also found a set of night vision goggles and three boxes of batteries to go with them. He tossed the goggles to Hasan, who took them with a smile.

They walked back past the shelves, making note of things they might need. "You know, it would almost be worth the convoy danger for the guys at the compound to come get all of this stuff," said Brad.

"Good idea, except this shop is in a bit of a bad neighborhood," Sean quipped back.

"Yeah, about that …" Brooks said as he dropped to the ground from the last rung of the ladder. "Looks like we'll be here for a while. I made it to the rooftop skylight; we're surrounded. I stopped counting at a hundred and fifty. But, from past experience, they get bored after a couple of days and go back to their nests."

"At least we are well provisioned," noted Hasan. He pointed at stacked cases of bottles of water and MREs.

The banging on the walls continued; it sounded like being in a small car in the middle of a hail storm. Occasionally it would let up, then the howl would sound and they would go back to the banging.

"Let's move these primal bodies out of the cage and against those sliding doors. Then we will pack up everything we want in the duffle bags and have them ready to go," said Sean. "Bring a couple cases of those MREs and the water in here. We're going to make all of our noise now and get it out of the way. I want everything packed and ready in the next thirty minutes. We're going to settle in the cage and wait for these bastards to go home. As long as we don't make any noise, they should get bored after a day or two."

Quickly the team dragged the primal bodies out of the cage and stacked them against the sliding doors. Brad searched the shelves, looking for what he thought he might need. Mostly he packed in MREs, but he also found a good multi tool and a couple of flashlights. He topped off his bag with a stack of first aid kits and some heavy leather work gloves. Brad moved back to the cleanest corner in the shelved-in area where the men had started settling in. Brooks moved back to the front of the building and verified the doors were secure before he pulled and locked the cage door behind them.

The men sat as quiet as possible for hours, and the moaning continued. It wasn't until late in the day that it finally began to die down. Even though the moaning had lessened, they could still hear the mass of them fumbling about outside the doors. Occasionally one of them would bang loudly against the steel door and wail in frustration. The team remained as silent as possible. When night came, they opened a box that contained some tarps and quietly spread them out on the floor to try to make the space more comfortable.

Brad watched Sean dig though his pack and pull out a worn and battered Iridium satellite phone. He pushed the power button but got no joy. He laid the phone on the tarp in front of him. Next to it, he placed the stack of batteries he'd salvaged from the cabinet. He tried the power on the new phone and it came to life with a ding. It showed a 20% power symbol and when Sean held the phone to his ear they could all hear the *'this phone is not active'* message. Sean quickly shut the phone off and removed the battery, then swapped it with the battery in his old phone. With the new battery now in place, Sean pressed the power button. They all saw the screen flash and the phone began to boot.

Sean waited for the phone to finish and the *'ready'* message appear on the LCD screen. He quickly entered the security password and unlocked the phone. All of the men sat up and watched intently as Sean cycled through the menu options. "So who do we call first?" Sean whispered. "How about we phone home in Kabul?" Sean pulled up the menu of stored phone numbers and cycled down. He found what he was looking for and pressed enter. The phone showed it was connected to the satellite and they heard the dialing and the ringing. It rang and rang until it received the automated message that the party they were calling was not available. So he tried Central Command in Bahrain, only to receive same message. Sean cycled through every number stored in the phone with the same result. Dejected, he tossed the phone to the tarp in front of him and sat back.

"Mind if I give it a try?" Brad asked.

"Have at it Brad, what's mine is yours," Sean replied.

Brad picked up the phone, dialed his family's number in Michigan, and pressed send. The phone dialed, connected, and began to ring on the other end. They all held their breath when a voice answered and Brad began to speak, but he was interrupted by an automated message:

This is the Emergency Broadcast System. The broadcasters in your area, in voluntary cooperation with the FCC and other authorities, have activated the emergency broadcast system. This system is to keep you informed in the event of an emergency. This is not a test, repeat, this is not a test. This is an actual emergency. Martial law has been declared in the greater territories of the United States. A 24-hour curfew has been put into effect. Based on the answering parties' area code you have been assigned to evacuation zone ... Blue 30. Your rally point is the intersection of ... Interstate 28 and US 41. Do not, repeat, do not attempt evacuation unless you are in immediate danger. Evacuation rally points will only be manned between the hours of noon and 2 p.m. Eastern Standard Time. Local law enforcement suggests rationing of food and water. Strongly encourage the avoidance of all non-family members. Do not leave your home unless you are attempting evacuation. Food drops will be made as soon as possible. Lethal force is authorized in defense of your dwelling or family members; local law enforcement cannot respond to calls for assistance. Tune to ... AM channel 1500 for news and updates.

As soon as the message finished, the call disconnected. Brad dialed the number again and intently listened to the broadcast a second time. He sat in silence for several minutes and listened to the primals outside milling about, banging into the sides of the building and occasionally letting loose with a moan. The sun had completely set now and there was no light coming in from the cracks in the steel roof. "What do you think, Sean?" Brad asked softly.

"I don't know. I mean, we went over the training scenarios before, you know for a U.S. invasion, but we never trained for anything like this. I would expect the martial law order, having people go into lock down; maybe it's a good thing, bro? Keeps people off the streets, maybe limits infection and the spread. Let's just keep hoping for the best till we hear otherwise, OK?" Sean answered.

"You know what, I have a number I want to try," Brooks said, reaching for the phone. He punched in a long number from memory ... the phone connected and dialed. After a moment they heard an answering machine.

"You have reached the coordinated voicemail message box; please leave your message after the beep."

"This is Team Member four zero two zero, team sierra oscar one, authentication number three six nine victor two seven, mission code zulu zulu." Brooks finished speaking into the phone and ended the call.

"What was that Brooks? Mind filling me in?" Sean queried.

"Hmm ... yeah ... from another life; several years ago working with the agency in the Balkans they gave me that drop number. We used to call in our stats four times a day, some things just stick in your memory, ya know," Brooks replied.

"And mission code zulu zulu?" Sean asked.

"Yeah, that means we are fucked, mission compromised, request immediate extraction. Hopefully they still monitor the box. I was told that it's processed by a team at Langley."

"Well, good thinking either way. Let's try to get some sleep while those things wander around out there, I'm sure we'll have another long day of waiting tomorrow."

8.

It was a long night; none of the men got much sleep. All through the evening they would be startled awake by a loud bang or the screeching of metal. Primals crashed against the steel walls and howled in frustration. Several times Brad woke from a dream, alarmed that the primals had breached the doors and were pouring through the cage walls, only to find them alone.

Brad tried to get comfortable without making too much noise. He found it difficult and he cursed himself for leaving the lucky unfired Sigma pistol back in his rucksack. He wouldn't make that mistake again. Tomorrow, he pledged to himself, he would find a place on his gear so he would always have it with him. He sat awake, staring at the sleeping men across from him, and wondered how the SEALs never had trouble passing out.

Morning came with an uneasy silence; the pounding had stopped with the dawn, and it had been hours since they'd heard a moan. Sean sent Brooks back up the ladder to peek outside. In the meantime, they opened MREs and had a cold, silent breakfast. Sean quietly opened a case of water and passed out bottles to the others. After a while, Brooks returned and took his seat back against the cage door. "Most of them are gone, but there's still about a half-dozen stubborn ones standing out there," Brooks whispered while opening a chicken fajita MRE. "I would say we're going to have to wait it out a bit longer; if we creep outside, one of them is sure to sound the alarm."

The men agreed and settled back into their rest spots to wait uncomfortably through the day. As morning passed, the temperature in the building went higher and higher. Soon it was over a hundred degrees inside and the heat, mixed with the stench of the dead primals and the mess that they had made in the void, made it a slow torture to sit there. Brad wrapped his scarf tightly around his head and tried to force himself to sleep to speed the time. He closed his eyes and began to dream about home.

He was at his parents' home sitting on the porch. The weather was perfect. Brad stepped off the porch into the fallen leaves and just stood there, enjoying the cool night air and the breeze on his face. His mother was at the flimsy screen door telling him to come back inside; his father told him it wasn't safe on the porch anymore. Brad didn't listen, the breeze comforted him. He had the Sigma pistol in his hand; he squeezed it, the grip cool against his palm. Brad liked the feel of the weapon. It was a heavy and full-framed pistol, built for war, and it made him feel safe holding it.

His mother pleaded for him to come back inside the house. Brad looked back at her and said he couldn't, he had to wait for him. "I can't leave him behind again," he said. "I'm sorry Mom, but I won't leave without him." Brad stepped onto the stone walkway, then calmly walked closer towards the tree line; looking intently into the shadows, he searched for his friend.

He heard the branches snapping in the woods that surrounded the house. Brad saw him cutting through the woods. It was dark and he couldn't make out the face, but he was sure it was him. Brad waved his hand to signal where he was. The man paused and turned towards him. The man waved back, changed direction and moved towards Brad.

Brad heard the howl of the wolves in the distance. Brad's father yelled for him to please get back in the house, but Brad ignored him too. He waved for the man in the woods to come closer. The man stepped out of the shadows; it was PFC Ryan! He waved back at Brad and smiled. Ryan was still wearing his full combat gear, and as he walked slowly toward the house, Brad saw Ryan's arm was covered with bloody bandages and his shoulder was twisted at a grotesque angle.

Brad's parents were yelling frantically now, pleading for him to return to the house ... but he shut out their voices. Not this close! He wouldn't leave him again. Brad looked beyond Ryan and saw the mob of primals crashing through the forest. The primal screams drowned out the sounds of everything else; it was all he could hear now. Brad screamed for Ryan to run to the house as he raised the Sigma pistol to fire.

Brad felt the sting on his cheek and the hand closed over his mouth. "You're making too much noise, buddy. You okay man?" Sean whispered. Brad woke from the dream and looked into the eyes of his friend; he nodded his head and Sean let go.

"It was just another bad dream," said Brad.

"No shame in that bro, we all got plenty of those coming to us," Sean whispered back before moving to his spot against the shelves.

Brad was covered in sweat. He opened his bottle and took a few quick swigs of the warm water. He looked at his watch; it was only 2 p.m., and yes, it was going to be another long day. As late afternoon came, a wind picked up and made the steel shell of the building rattle. Even though it startled the team inside, it didn't affect the primals outside at all. In no way did they seem to care about the slap of the steel roof or the snapping of tent flaps outside. They had a very 'in-tune' filter that knew the difference between what was a natural sound and what was prey.

Brad whispered to Sean and asked if it would be okay if he took a look out through the roof skylight. When Sean nodded his approval, Brad silently rose and stretched to relieve himself of the cramps in his body. He left his rifle next to his duffle bag full of scavenged goods, walked through the cage door and to the ladder. He stealthily climbed the rungs until he reached the small landing at the top. Easing himself off the ladder, he took a seat next to the skylight, slowly opened the window, and peered outside. As Brooks had said, there were still six of them standing in that meditative state, motionless in the roadway leading to the supply building. Brad looked around as far as he could. From his position on the top of the building, he had a better vantage point of the camp than he had the day before.

He scanned all around. Off in the distance, he could see the living area where his tent had been. He wondered if his personal belongings were still there: his pictures of family, the letters from home. *Even if they are*, he thought, *I can't risk my team to go after them.*

The sun was starting to set in the sky and the things standing watch on the road were starting to move again. The primals seemed oblivious to him high up on the roof. Brad watched as others woke and walked out of the tents and bunkers that covered the camp. Just as he had seen in the desert, they would stand and sniff the air, then slowly gather. When they had formed a pack of about a dozen they would wander off in search of prey. He observed them doing this all over the camp. He realized with a sinking feeling that Bremmel must be home to over a thousand of the primals by now.

As the sun went completely into the horizon and night fell, the howling started and he could hear them moving about. Brad had left his goggles below with his gear, so he could no longer see them clearly. He looked below where he knew the six primals stood watch but he could no longer make out their forms. Brad slowly closed the window and descended the ladder back into the warehouse. Moving silently, he made his way back into the cage and locked it behind him. He sat on his gear and stretched his legs out in front of him. Brad considered eating as he saw his other teammates had begun to do, but he was certain he wouldn't be able to hold down his food tonight with the overwhelming stench surrounding them. Instead, he again wrapped the scarf tightly around his head and fell into a dreamless sleep.

9.

He was startled awake by the sound of Brooks closing the cage door. "All clear," he said. "There are a couple of them in that Zen state about a hundred meters out, but we should be able to drop them with no problem," Brooks finished.

"Okay fellas, I recommend you drain your bladders and take in as much water as you can hold. Let's be ready to move out in ten minutes," Sean told the team. "We're going to make as direct a path as possible toward the gates. If you see personnel on the ground, we'll stop for quick ammo collection but that's it."

"There are sealed cans of ammo in the guard shack, near the gate," Brad said.

Sean gave him a puzzled look.

"Sorry, I forgot about that earlier," Brad explained. "But I know where it's at and I can grab it on the way out," he added.

Sean nodded and they lifted their heavy bags of goods to their backs. When they were all stacked on the door, Brooks unbolted and slowly opened it.

Just as he'd said, the outside was clear of primals. Silently, Brooks moved in a crouched run to the nearest barrier, his footfalls barely making a noise. He lifted his hand to point out the two meditating primals at the end of the street. Calling his men to a halt, they all took a knee while Brooks and Sean, in perfect timing, took synchronized shots that dropped the two. They listened intently to make sure they hadn't alerted any of the sleeping lions before they got back to their feet and moved toward the gate.

They moved quickly and silently without stopping until they arrived just short of the exit. Brooks again put his fist in the air, calling the group to a halt. He pointed at Brad and called him to his position up front. "Where's this guard shack?" Brooks asked.

"Right there, next to the wall," Brad pointed to a spot less than a hundred meters away. Alone and against the 'T' wall sat a plywood structure with Plexiglas windows. Sandbags covered the walls halfway up, and they were also stacked along the roof. From a distance, the structure appeared empty.

"Okay, go clean it out, the shack looks empty from here," Sean whispered, looking through his scope at the guard shack.

As Brad started to move towards the shack, he looked behind him and saw that Hasan was following. He nodded his approval to the man. Brad stopped just short of the shack and then signaled to Hasan that he was going to open the door and peek inside. Brad walked the last few feet to the door and slowly turned the handle and pushed on the door. When it was opened just a crack he looked inside. He saw a decomposing uniformed soldier crumpled on the floor, his corpse blocking the door. Brad slowly put his weight against the door, pushing and sliding the man's body out of the way. When he was able to finally enter the shack, he felt a deepening sense of grief as he looked down at the dead soldier. Even though he didn't recognize the man, the body represented everyone he had lost. He quickly shoved the feelings aside and sucked it up.

He pushed the door the rest of the way and stepped over the soldier. He found the ammo cans in an unlocked locker, right where he remembered them to be stored from his time on guard duty. Brad lifted all four cans of rifle ammo from the trunk, then another two cans of the pistol ammo. Hasan stepped forward and tied a rope through the handles of three of the cans and lifted them to his back. Brad did the same with the last three cans and they moved back towards the team.

They linked back up with Brooks and Sean and followed them out through the gate and onto the road. As they put some distance on the gate, Brad felt his levels of anxiety begin to fade. Brooks guided them rapidly down the road and to the large formation of rocks where they had hidden the vehicle. Brad was relieved when he rounded the corner and saw it sitting there just as they had left it. He had been nervous that the primals might have torn it apart or some other survivors may have driven off with it during the night. Wasting no time, they stowed their duffel bags of gear and the thousands of rifle and pistol rounds salvaged from the guard shack. After a last, careful look all the way around, they boarded the Defender and Brooks started the engine. He backed them up and pulled the vehicle onto the road, speeding away from Forward Operating Base Bremmel, the camp that now housed an army of primals. Brad glanced back one last time at his old home, knowing that he'd never see it again.

The vehicle bounced on the rough road. Brooks kept his speed slow enough so that he could safely navigate the potholes and abandoned vehicles that occasionally blocked his path. They drove silently until they were back at the intersection to the Hairatan road. Brooks stopped the vehicle in the middle of the street and looked at Sean.

"Well gentlemen, we seem to be at a cross road. Do we continue or head back?" Sean asked.

"We go forward," Hasan answered sharply.

"Bro, if we go back, I don't think I will ever leave that compound again. Let's just keep moving until this is over with," Brad said.

"I go where you go," Brooks said, looking at Sean.

"Well, start it up and let's get moving," Sean said as he fastened his seat belt.

They drove forward and passed the Hairatan road. After a while they passed a sign that indicated "*Kholm 40km*". Sean pointed to the sign. "What do you know of this place, Hasan?" he asked as they passed by.

"Kholm? The town is Tajik, they are farm people, and they keep to themselves," Hasan said. "They have a good market, but there is little else in the city. I suggest we skip the city and go to Aybak instead. If you will stay on this road, and continue out of the city, it will only be another couple of hours. I know a place we may be able to seek shelter. There is a safe house that is known to me outside the village on the main road," he finished.

"Very good. Brooks, you heard the man, follow the road," Sean said with a smile.

As the vehicle sped along, Sean reached into his pack and pulled out the satellite phone. Then he pulled out the box the new phone had come in. Digging through the box, he found what he was looking for, grabbing a long twisted cord and a charger for the phone. He plugged one end into the phone, the other into the vehicle, and heard a beep as a green light indicated the battery was charging. "And now as long as we have this ride we can charge our phone," Sean laughed.

The vehicle continued on and entered the city of Kholm. They stuck to the main road, being careful to go around abandoned vehicles. To the sides, they could see the same signs of struggle and violence they had witnessed in Hairatan. Many of the storefronts were burned out; there were corpses on the sidewalks. The city was eerily quiet and they had yet to spot a primal in the city limits.

Brooks drove slowly as he weaved through the idle traffic, braking only if he had to drive over a curb to avoid a downed vehicle or a barrier. Kholm was small and it didn't take long to clear the city center. As they began to pull away, they heard the *crack, crack, crack* of automatic gunfire. Alarmed, they all began to look around but saw nothing. A loud metallic impact smacked the vehicle; a hole appeared in the back of the cab, and another pierced the rear window, spiderwebbing it.

"Floor it!" Sean yelled to Brooks as he lowered his window and readied his rifle. Brooks gunned the vehicle and they raced away down the road, taking no more shots as they left the city behind.

"What was that, Hasan?" Sean shouted.

"Kholm is obviously not a friendly place these days. They can be very territorial. If you ask me, that was a warning," Hasan said. "If they had wanted us dead, they would have ambushed us on the road into the city. Those were warning shots; they let us clear the city and gave warning for us not to return," he continued.

"Fair enough, but if they shoot at me again I will park this car and sneak into that shithole in the middle of the night. They will have more to worry about than just the primals!" Sean snapped back.

They continued down the highway and once again found themselves on open road. The terrain was rockier and more mountainous here than it had been in the north.

"Where is this hideout of yours?" Sean asked.

"Soon you will see it, but we still have a ways to drive," Hasan answered, then leaned back into the seat and lowered his hat to cover his eyes while he drifted to sleep. Brad watched Hasan and liked the idea of sleep. He stared out his side window and watched the terrain go by. Dwellings and ruins were growing closer and closer together as they entered the heart of the country. Soon, he too had drifted to sleep, lulled by the sound of the purring tires on pavement.

When Brad woke, the Defender was pulled to the shoulder of the road. There were high mountains on both sides and the sun was still shining brightly. Brad lowered his window and called to Sean, who was leaning against the side of the truck.

"What's up? Why did we stop?"

"Nature calls, brother," Sean answered back, pointing to Brooks perched behind a set of large rocks.

Brad undid his seat belt and opened his door; he was drenched in sweat from his road nap. He reached into his bag and pulled out a water bottle. After opening it, he drained what was left of the warm liquid. Hasan walked up from the other side of the vehicle, then stopped, took a seat up on the hood, and perched his rifle in his lap.

"So, how much further to your safe house, Hasan?" Brad questioned.

"Not much further, just over these hills and on the approach to Aybak," Hasan replied, not looking up from his rifle.

Brad took a long look around. They were in a valley; the ground had gotten very hard and this gave him a comfortable feeling knowing there were fewer dunes for the primals to rise out of. He walked to the back of the vehicle and examined the two holes there courtesy of the trip through Kholm. He went back to his bag, grabbed a large roll of green duct tape, and plugged the holes. He placed a large amount on the spiderwebbed hole in the glass to try and keep it from breaking further. When he was finished, he noticed Sean and Brooks had made their way back to their seats in the Defender. Brad took that as an indication that their rest stop had ended and moved back to his position in the vehicle.

The mountains had grown high and there were even patches of green appearing on both sides of the winding road as they drove further south. They started to come across several stone buildings and even an occasional mosque. But there were no signs of life, or if there was any life, they were hiding it very well. As they passed over a large hill, Hasan signaled for Brooks to move off of the road and onto a small trail that broke east away from the highway. The trail was nothing more than a heavily rutted goat path that wound down and into the boulder-strewn terrain.

Out of the terrain, smaller homes started to pop up. They were very old and most were crumbled—many without roofs.

"This village has been abandoned since the Russians came," Hasan spoke. "Occasionally some families will live here during migrations to the river, but for the most part it is always a ghost town.

"At the end of this trail, go to the right; our house sits at the top of the hill against the mountain," Hasan said to Brooks while pointing.

Brooks eased the vehicle down the winding trail, careful to avoid rocks or large dips in the road. At the top of the hill was a stone-walled home. It was very small, unlike the villa they had stayed at on the Hairatan road. The house settled into a very high mountain slope and faced an open view of the terrain below. It appeared to be carved into the side of the mountain, as were other homes they saw when looking at neighboring dwellings.

They could see that all of the homes in the area did indeed look uninhabited. Surprisingly, there was grass and vegetation in the area and a mountain stream cut a path down through the back of the empty village. This home had obviously been kept up by someone. Brad was surprised that the coalition forces would miss it, but then again it was far off the trail and you could not see its condition until being on top of it.

Brooks pulled the vehicle in close to the stone wall and positioned it behind a pile of stacked boulders to hide it from any approaching vehicles. The men stepped out of the Defender, stretched, listened, and tried to remain quiet until they were sure they were alone. After several minutes, Sean readied his rifle and approached the house. Hasan indicated that he would check the home first.

"It is often left booby trapped. I should go first and clear the way," Hasan whispered to Sean as he stepped forward and headed to the house.

The wall here was badly damaged. Although it wrapped all the way around the home until it ended in the face of the mountain, its height varied from one to four feet at its highest point. The door to the home was made of planks, but Hasan did not use it. Instead, he went to the window and moved his hand slowly along the sill. Finding a wire, he traced his hand back to the corner of the windowsill and, from within a carefully carved hole, removed an old Russian-style grenade. He pulled a pin from his shirt collar and attached it to the head of the grenade. He then grabbed a rubber band from his pocket and carefully wrapped it around the spoon, then placed the grenade on the ground at the base of the window. Next, Hasan leaned his rifle against the wall and pulled the 9mm pistol he had found at Bremmel from his pack, then slipped into the home through the window. After countless uncomfortable minutes, the door unlatched and opened outwards. Hasan walked through the open doorway and retrieved his rifle. "This home, as you would say, is clear," Hasan said with a smile.

The team gathered their packs and secured the vehicle before moving into the house. They found one large communal room with a fireplace along the back wall which rested against the mountain. Sean went to set his pack down when Hasan grinned at him and said, "Not yet, my friend." Hasan put on his backpack, dropped to his belly, and crawled into the open mouth of the fireplace. Rising slightly, he disappeared into the back of it.

Sean just looked at Brooks and Brad with a puzzled expression.

"Well, what the hell," Brooks said as he put on his own pack and followed Hasan through the hole. Sean went next, then Brad. After a very tight squeeze thorough the mouth of the fireplace, they also traversed the high step up into the chimney and found the tunnel that Hasan had disappeared into. They had to crawl another fifteen feet directly into the mountain before the tunnel opened into a large cavern. When Brad exited the tunnel, he rolled to his side and Brooks helped pull him to his feet.

They found Hasan at the center of the cavern, lighting lanterns and tossing stacked wood into a fire pit.

"What do you think, my friends? Afghan engineering at its best, yes?" he said with a big smile. "You can place your things over there." Hasan pointed to a large area carved into the wall that was filled with cots.

"I am very impressed, Hasan," Brooks said. "This is not the first time I have ventured into one of your caves, but this is the first time I have been a welcome guest." He walked towards the cots and tossed his heavy bag onto one before moving back to the pit and helping Hasan with building a fire.

Brad looked around the room, walked to the center and, finding a stool, sat down. "You are full of surprises, Hasan," he said. "How many places like this are there?"

"More than I can count, my friend," Hasan answered.

With the fire growing hot, Brad watched the smoke lift to the top of the high cavern and drift farther into the mountain.

"How far does the tunnel go back?" he questioned.

"I am not sure. I have been deep in the mountain, but never to the end of the passage. There were limits to where I was allowed to venture," Hasan said.

He then got to his feet and lifted a large iron pot from a stone shelf. After placing the pot in the coals, he used bottles of water from his pack to fill it. "There is a spring in the back of the cave that flows from the river for water, we can refill these bottles before we leave," Hasan said while working. He then walked back to the stone shelf and lifted the cover from a large clay vase, from which he removed several heaping bowls full of a rice and bean mixture to add to the iron pot.

As the water boiled, Hasan added spices and a large bundle of dried meat that he removed from his pack. "After two nights in that steel building, we deserve a hearty meal," Hasan said to the group.

"How do you know of this place, Hasan?" Sean asked.

Hasan smiled and sat on a bench near the pot before telling his story.

"I first came here when I was a boy; my father used to bring me here. We would come to the village often to trade his livestock for goods. In those days, people lived in the village at the base of the hill, but the Russians changed that because of a disagreement between the elders and the local commander. The village fell quickly out of favor with the Russians and it was burnt. The mujahedeen rebuilt this home and a few others. I don't know how long the passage to the cavern has existed. My father talked of visiting it when he was a child, so I imagine the house was built around the entrance.

"After this place was destroyed, the people left. The next village was beyond walking distance from our home, so we lost our ability to safely trade our livestock. My father was angry at the loss of our trade and our friends so he took up arms against the Russians. Weeks later, I walked the road from our home to this now empty village with my father and two older brothers. My father negotiated a trade with the mujahedeen commander. My father gave the best of our flock in exchange for rifles and ammunition. Purchasing our own weapons gave us independence. In those days, if a mujahedeen commander gifted you a weapon, he then owned you, and you were a member of his force. My father, by purchasing weapons of his own, was able to freelance, I believe you would say.

"We traveled the road often after that. Sometimes the mujahedeen would pay us to do missions for them. Mostly we helped lead foreign fighters to cross the Amu Darya River from the borders of Uzbekistan and Tajikistan. And even sometimes your own CIA would come here with our help; business was good for us. When the Russians left, my father retired our small force, and my brothers and I tried to return to the village life. But the peace did not last for long. After the Taliban took control of the government, my father was urged to rejoin the fight. He took all of his sons with him and we traveled to the northeast and joined the Alliance. My father was killed in a skirmish with the Pakistanis soon after. Later, I lost both of my brothers to a suicide bomber.

"I stayed with the Alliance for many years, even after the death of our leader. I even supported the U.S. invasion, but soon after the U.S. forces arrived the Alliance broke up in the name of a new, weakened government. So I returned to my home in the village. I tried to adapt to the new ways of peace and forced prosperity.

"The roadside bombings started the spring after I returned home. We had nothing to do with the insurgents in our area; nonetheless, our elders were labeled as collaborators. The helicopters came in the night and left with many of our village leaders. Soon I found myself back in these caverns again, doing what I knew best. I was on a hired mission working for a cell in Hairatan when this new enemy attacked my people.

"I was far north of the border arranging delivery of rockets to be shipped to the Taliban when word reached me. My first instincts were to get home to my family, but I soon realized that would be impossible. I discovered most of the roads to be impassable, and in the early hours the streets and highways were flooded with the hordes of walking monsters. I fled with others to the hills. We were not armed north of the border, and our primary defense was to become faster than those who traveled with us.

"I made my way to the banks of the river, and I was able to barter with a boatman for passage across. By sticking to the high ground, I was able to avoid the mobs and make my way back to Hairatan. I met Junayd in a safe house east of the city. We were known to each other by reputation alone, but we do not share the same principles. We agreed to work together only for reasons of self-preservation." As Hasan finished, he reached forward to stir the boiling contents of the pot.

"What do you know of your family?" Brad asked.

"In the first day my cell phone operated, but there was mass chaos. My wife was confused and didn't know where to go. I was able to negotiate with a cell member in the area who promised to keep them safe. Unfortunately, the phones stopped working before I could confirm that she had been rescued. I have to admit that it is selfish motives that brought me to join you on your venture. My wife and child do not live in this region. I moved them near the main airbase years ago. I joined you in hopes of finding information on their wellbeing," Hasan answered solemnly. Brad just hung his head in sad thought as Sean stood and extended his hand to Hasan.

"We are happy to have you on our team, brother; you have already proven yourself useful, thank you," Sean said.

"Very good then. Let's feast tonight on real food. After two nights in the steel building we deserve a good meal, and not the mess that comes from the cans that Brad feeds us," said Hasan with a grin.

10.

After they finished eating, Sean told Brad that they needed to go outside and set up security. The front had been left unattended way longer than it should have been. Because of the tunnel and isolation of the watch station, they had decided the watch would be two men at all times in the home. Brad readied his rifle and followed Sean into the tunnel. The sun had started to go down and the tunnel had grown dark with most of the ambient light from the house gone. Sean exited first and took a knee just outside and waited for Brad to post up next to him. They sat for a few minutes listening to make sure they were alone. Then Sean rose to his feet and moved to the window. Brad came up behind him and they both scanned the horizon. The sky was orange and they probably had less than an hour of daylight left.

"I need to get some gear out of the Defender before we lose the light," Sean said.

"Okay boss, I can observe you from here," Brad replied.

Sean walked out through the door and moved to the vehicle. It could be seen easily from the house, but was near invisible from the road or the small trail that approached the home. Brad looked beyond the vehicle and saw that the shadows over the ruins of the village had started to stretch. He hated this time of the day, when the sun seemed to move quickly and the shifting shadows could play tricks on your mind. More than once he thought he spotted a primal staring at him, only to look through his binos and find a boulder or a long ago knocked-over wall.

Brad turned his attention back to Sean. It looked like he had finished what he was doing and was locking up the Defender. Sean threw a bag over his shoulder and started the walk back to the house. As he entered the doorway, he dropped his bag before securing the old rusty bolts at the top and bottom of the plank door.

"You get what you needed Sean?" Brad asked.

"Yeah, grabbed up a couple thousand rounds of ammo from the cans you picked up. I got to thinking how it would suck to get surrounded and have all the ammo sitting out there in the truck," Sean said.

"Damn, good thinking! Guess that's why you're the chief," Brad said with a grin.

Brad found a chair and set it to the back of the window in the shadows, but still in position to where he could see out. Sean began pulling items from his bag and laying them out on a table in the center of the room. He sat his MK11 sniper rifle on the table, and two extra magazines next to it, but kept his suppressed MP5 across his chest where it hung from a tactical sling.

Brad turned his attention back to the ruins and watched as the orange light began to fade into a deep grey. Far in his peripheral he sensed motion. Brad stood and took a step closer to the window, still being very careful to stay concealed. He lifted his binos and scanned the lower quarter of the village where he thought he had seen something. He watched for a moment.

"What do you got, Brad?" Sean asked.

"Nothing yet, but I thought I saw something."

"Got to be careful, buddy, these twilight shadows can play tricks on you," Sean said.

"I know, but it looked like movement ... oh wait, there it is again," Brad exclaimed.

With new interest, Sean got to his feet and stepped to the window. Brad, using his hand in a karate chop motion, pointed out the direction where he thought he had seen something.

"Well, what exactly did you see Brad?" Sean asked.

"I can't be sure, but it looked like a group of people running," Brad answered. "There! See them? By the low wall." He pointed.

"I got them, three targets moving left to right," Sean said, barely above a whisper and reaching for his rifle. "Wait, those aren't primals. They appear to be one male adult, one female adult, one child," he continued emotionlessly. "They just dropped into the ruins of that house, third from the left on the trail head, about 550 meters."

"What are they doing here?" Brad asked.

"Oh shit, I got two primals tracking them. I don't think they have a fix on the friendly position yet; they're walking, not running. Primals moving left to right 700 meters out," Sean whispered.

"You want me to go get Brooks?" Brad asked apprehensively.

"No, not yet. Get on your scope, fire up the night vision—I need a spotter," Sean answered. "Do you see the primals? They are just off the trail, moving at a walk."

"Okay I got them," Brad whispered. "Are you going to take the shot?"

"No, too dangerous," Sean answered. "If we fire now, we might get every primal this side of the mountain knocking on both of our doors."

"Yeah, I guess that wouldn't be good for anyone," Brad whispered back.

The two watched through their scopes as the primals tracked the group. They observed them stalking the trail, stopping every so often to sniff at the air. "They seem to be evolving. Look at how they're hunting them," Sean whispered.

The primals continued to walk down the trail toward the hiding spot. When they got to within fifty feet of the house, one of them dropped back and investigated something on the side of the trail. The lead primal was more aware; he continued down the trail, stopping where it broke to a walkway that led up to the ruined home. It halted in the middle of the path, sniffing at the air and examining the ground. Brad watched the lead primal walk right at the hiding group's position. Just short of the entryway to the house, he stopped and again put his nose to the air before continuing forward.

Brad had the dot of his scope on the body of the creature as it crossed the threshold of the ruined home. Without warning, he saw the female rise to her feet just in front of the creature. Brad watched intently, waiting and expecting to hear the primal moan as it called to the other crazy. Brad watched the creature raise its hand and arch its back, preparing to lunge at the female. Brad had his finger on the trigger. Noise or not, he wouldn't watch another human be taken without a fight. But before a sound left its mouth, the male stepped from a shadow behind the primal and removed its head with a shining blade. As soon as it started, both friendlies had again vanished, and nothing was left but the corpse of the primal.

"Things just got interesting," Sean whispered.

They continued watching as the second primal regained its bearings and turned toward the house. It was moving slowly, occasionally stopping to sniff the air. It eventually found the house and turned to the entryway. Brad again watched this one walk through the doorway and stop when it found the downed primal. With no signs of alarm, it just stopped and put its nose to the air. This only lasted a second as the male again stepped from the shadows and with a quick swing separated the primal from its head.

"Who the hell are they?" Brad asked.

"Got me, but they have their shit together for sure," Sean answered.

After a short wait, the two men watched the group again break cover. The woman was carrying the child and the man had all of the bags. They moved quickly to a ruin two houses away and disappeared into their surroundings once more. It was now pitch black. Even with a partial moon in a clear sky, you couldn't make out anything with the naked eye.

"What do you make of this?" Brad asked.

"I don't know, but it just made more work for us," Sean said. "Make sure you keep an eye on those ruins."

"I got them, but do you think we should go down there? Maybe we can help them with something," Brad said.

"No way, I like my head, and that man down there seems to be pretty proficient in removing them," Sean answered. "For now let's just observe them. If they are still there in the morning we'll talk it over."

Now that it was completely dark, Brad moved his seat forward and rested the handguard of the rifle on the windowsill. He had the binos high to his eyes, and was watching the ruins where he'd seen the group disappear. The trio was very quiet, and Brad and Sean wouldn't even have known they existed if they hadn't been on watch to witness the evening's events. Brad looked to his left and saw that Sean also had his eye on his scope, scanning the horizon. Far away they could see the road; it was very dark, and even through the night vision it was hard to make out any movement. Brad and Sean settled in and watched.

Just after midnight they heard a noise coming from inside the tunnel. Brad turned to see Brooks crawl out, followed by Hasan. They quietly briefed the men on what had happened earlier and pointed out the location of the group using the IR laser on Sean's rifle. When they were satisfied their relief was current on the situation, they dropped to their bellies and crawled back through the tunnel and into the cavern.

The cave still had the lantern burning where Hasan had left it. The fire still smoked, its coals burning a bright orange, eerily lighting the area. Brad moved off to the sleeping area where he had placed his belongings earlier. He opened his bedroll and rolled it out across an old dusty bunk. As he lay down, he noticed writing on the stone walls above him. It looked to be a long list of names. It made him wonder how many young fighters had slept on this bunk, waiting to face the war outside. Brad smiled to himself, then reached into his bag for a sharpie and added his name to the bottom of the list.

11.

Sean was already up and messing with the fire when Brad awoke. He'd opened two cans of the Afghan slop and had it simmering in a pot. The stench had already begun to fill the cavern. Sean looked over as he noticed Brad stirring in his bedroll.

"Good morning, sunshine. I found some tea and there's hot water if you want some. It's almost 4 a.m. and I want to get moving soon if you can manage to get your ass up," he said half-jokingly.

"I'm up, I'm up. Hell, how could anyone sleep through the smell of that shit?" Brad retorted.

Sean put on his vest and lifted his rifle. He walked to the tunnel entrance and indicated he was going to relieve Brooks for breakfast, and that Brad should do the same with Hasan when he was ready. Brad took a long drink off of his water bottle, then walked to the kettle on the bench and filled it with the Afghan tea. He found the tea bitter but acceptable, especially with no other source of caffeine nearby. Brooks crawled through the opening of the cavern just as he was getting himself a bowl of the slop. "So any change on our neighbors?" Brad asked.

"Nope, no movement at all. I didn't see them slip away during the night, so they must be dug in and hiding good."

"Yeah, I guess for them to have survived this long alone, they would have to be good at hiding," Brad said. "That guy is good with his steel also; I watched him remove those primals' heads with one swing."

"Well let's hope he's friendly, I'd hate to have to put him down," Brooks said, filling a bowl full of the slop.

Brad finished his breakfast and crawled back through the tunnel opening and into the house. He gave Hasan a pat on the back to let him know he was relieved, then took a seat in the corner. He saw Sean sitting in the window silently observing the ruins of the village. He looked at his watch and figured they still had maybe thirty minutes till dawn.

"I got movement," Sean whispered.

Brad got to his feet and took a spot just over Sean's shoulder and lifted his binos.

In the area where the group had disappeared, they could see the flickering glow of a fire and a small trail of smoke going into the sky. "Must be meal time," Sean whispered.

There was very little sign of movement other than the smoke. They watched as suddenly the male figure broke cover and climbed out of the ruin. He stood silently looking for danger. They could tell by his movement that he had experience in the wild. He appeared comfortable as he began to move toward the river with the large, empty water bladders.

The sun was starting to break the horizon and they could easily observe the man now without the aid of night vision. He disappeared from their view as he dropped down to the river, but was back within a few minutes. He had the two water bladders tied end to end and hanging over his neck; they also could see he carried a large sword in a sheath strapped across his back. When he got closer to the ruin, they watched the child run out and greet the man with a hug. Then the woman came from behind the child and took the water bladders from the man.

"Hmm. They seem friendly enough; let's keep an eye on them. When Hasan gets back we'll go talk to them," Sean whispered.

They heard a noise behind them. Brad turned and, as if they had been part of the conversation, Hasan and Brooks crawled out of the tunnel carrying all the gear. They lifted their heavy bags and sat them next to the door.

"The neighbors are up," Sean said to Brooks in a low voice.

Brooks stepped to the window and took a peek out. "Looks like a family. What's the plan, boss?"

"I was thinking you and Hasan could take a step out to greet them, your Dari is better than mine, and I'm sure Hasan has us both beat," Sean said with a chuckle.

"We should leave our weapons; we don't want to startle them. I'm sure we are more than safe with these gentlemen's rifles on us," Hasan said. He stepped to the table and laid his newly found M9 pistol and the worn AK on the wooden face. Brooks looked uneasy, but reluctantly placed his weapons on the table as well. Before stepping away, he turned back and picked up the MK23 pistol, tucking it into his shirt.

"Sorry Hasan, I can't go outside buck naked," he said.

They went to the door and walked out. Sean and Brad watched them move away from the house and through the small yard. They passed through the gate of the low stone wall and by the Defender.

"I have the male, you have the female," Sean whispered.

Brad cringed and placed the red dot of his scope on the body of the female; she was still blissfully unaware of the approach of Brooks and Hasan. Brad watched her preparing the morning meal; she looked to be removing grains from a bag and adding them to a pot on the fire.

When Hasan had moved several paces from the Defender, he stopped in the center of the road and raised his hands. Brad could tell that he was saying something just loud enough for the family to hear, but Brad couldn't tell what from his location. The woman quickly got to her feet and grabbed the child; then she scurried back to the safety of the ruin and disappeared from sight. Brad moved the rifle and changed focus to the male, who now had the sword unsheathed and was pointing it in the direction of Brooks and Hasan. From the man's body language, Brad could tell he was shouting warnings.

He watched as Brooks and Hasan closed the distance on the man, the woman still hidden from sight. Both team members held their hands in the air and showed their empty palms to the man. There seemed to be an intense discussion before the man finally lowered his sword. Hasan stepped forward first and continued the conversation with the man. Brad could tell by their movements that the tone had improved. Then Hasan turned and motioned Brooks forward. After a few more minutes and the exchanging of handshakes, Hasan pointed at the house and the man looked in their direction. Brooks looked up and gave them a hand sign that it was clear to come down.

"We're up," Sean said.

He took his rifle and slung it across his back. Then he lifted the MP5 and clipped it to a ring on the front of his vest. Brad did the same with his rifle and then followed Sean out the door.

"So what is our plan with these people?" Brad asked.

"Let's not get ahead of ourselves. For now this is just about gathering intel. Our plans haven't changed and we'll be moving out very soon."

They walked down the trail and approached the ruins of the house. The woman was back out of her hide now, but stayed back in the ruins and eyed the men suspiciously. Brad saw the child, a small boy, staring at him. Brad made a face at the boy and smiled. The boy laughed and smiled back. The woman took notice of Brad's gesture and seemed to relax a bit.

Sean stepped forward and shook hands with the man, then attempted to look relaxed by leaning against the wall of the house. Brad took up a spot just a bit further away where he could still observe the surrounding area, conscious that this was not a safe spot.

"This is Farid and his wife; the boy is his nephew," Hasan said. "They fled from a village many miles from here and have been moving for weeks."

"What do they know of the south?" Sean asked.

Hasan asked the man the question, to which he made a sour face as he replied.

"He says the roads are very dangerous, the cities are to be avoided. Farid says that the south holds many more of the creatures than we have seen here," Hasan said. "He says there are large armies of the creatures in the south; the roads are choked with them. He says he and his wife only travel by the mountain trails."

The man continued speaking and his voice became more desperate. "He is asking for our help. He asked for us to take his nephew with us," Hasan said.

Sean smiled at the man and stepped forward, putting a hand on his shoulder. "Hasan, tell Farid about the survivors in Hairatan. Tell him about the cavern behind the house. Tell him we will get them settled in today, but we cannot take him or the boy with us," said Sean.

Hasan relayed the message; the man showed a face of concern, and then spoke urgently to Hasan. "He is pleading with us," Hasan said.

"Ask them to gather their belongings. We'll show them the house and its provisions; I'm sure this will ease his worries," Sean said. "Hasan, you do understand that we do not have room for these people, don't you?"

"Yes, I understand my friend, but I also take great pleasure in that being a decision which I do not have to make," Hasan answered.

They helped the family gather their belongings after they had finished eating, then led them to the top of the hill towards the house. Apprehensively they entered the small house and Hasan showed them the entrance to the cave. Brooks elected to remain outside and stand watch as the rest of them entered the cavern.

Hasan showed them the fire pit and the clay vases filled with beans and rice. He showed them the sleeping areas and the small containers of oil for the lamps, and the spot where fresh water flowed into the cave. Lastly, Hasan walked them to a corner of the cavern's main room and removed some earth from the floor; lifting a panel, he revealed a small hole. In the hole were several objects wrapped in oil cloth. Hasan pulled one out and removed the cloth to reveal an old and worn AK74 rifle. It was a smaller variant of the AK47 designed to fire a lighter round. Hasan handed the rifle to the man, and then kneeling he reached farther into the hole, grabbing three magazines and two large bandoleers of ammunition. Then he closed the wood cover and moved earth back to conceal the hole.

He set the ammunition on a table next to the man, then asked if he was familiar with the weapon; the man nodded to indicate that he was. Hasan placed his hands on the man's shoulder and spoke to him reassuringly, then removed some paper from his pocket and wrote the man a note, which the man read and then squeezed in his fist. Looking at Brad and Sean, Hasan said "We should gather our belongings; we should get on the road soon."

Brad and Sean gathered the rest of the gear, taking notice that the woman was already rearranging the furniture in the cavern as they prepared to exit. Brad lifted his bag to his shoulder but Farid stepped forward and took the pack from him and then headed for the tunnel exit. Brad turned to smile and wave at the boy who returned the gesture, and then he lowered himself into the exit. They carried their gear to the vehicle and strapped everything down tightly. Farid helped to attach Brad's bag to the roof racks and made sure it was completely lashed down; then he spoke at Brad in words he didn't understand, and extended his hand.

They all shook hands and wished the man luck as they boarded the vehicle. Hasan walked the man back to the house, and Brad observed him showing the man the Russian grenade on the ground and giving an explanation of how to set up the booby trap. He watched the men smile and hug goodbye before Hasan walked back to the Defender. Silently he took his seat and Brooks pulled the Defender out of its hide and back onto the trail.

They rode in silence until they hit the main road and the Defender picked up speed.

"What was on the note?" Brad asked Hasan.

"I wrote him an order, it indicated to all that Farid was a caretaker for the house and cavern. I gave him notice that it would be his responsibility to assist refugees on the road, and to keep the cavern maintained until we returned for them," Hasan said.

"And if we don't return?" asked Brooks.

"Then that would indicate that I am dead, but at least the family will still be living in the cavern," Hasan answered.

12.

They continued down Route A76 heading south and deeper into Afghanistan. The sun was climbing higher in the sky and they passed more and more homes. The countryside became more populated, which also increased their sightings of wandering primals. Often they would slow to bypass a barrier or a blocked vehicle, only to hear the howling. Brooks would make his way around the blockade and pick up speed just as the primals came into sight.

"I hope those bastards don't follow us," Brad said.

"Let them follow. They will have a long ass walk ahead of them; we need to make good time today, fellas," Sean answered back.

They settled in and Brooks kept the vehicle moving at a good speed, considering the quality of the road. Just as Brad considered nodding off, they heard a buzzing sound.

"What is that?" Brad asked as the *buzz buzz buzz* continued.

"Oh shit," Sean yelled, startled as he started ripping at his day pack. "It's the Sat phone."

Brooks hit the brakes and pulled to the side of the road just as Sean found the phone and pressed the green 'answer' button.

"Hello, hello," Sean said into the receiver. "Oh, yes, just a second." He pulled the phone from his ear and handed it to Brooks. "It's for you."

Brooks grabbed the phone and put it to his ear. "Yes, this is team member four zero two zero. Oh yeah ... my authentication number is three six nine victor two seven. Hell *yeah* it's been a long time! Who is this? Hold on, I am here with three others, I'm placing the phone on speaker ... I have SEAL team Chief Sean Rogers, Staff Sergeant Brad Thompson, and one local national with me."

"Hello? Can you hear me?" came the voice from the phone.

"Loud and clear. Who is speaking?" Sean asked.

"This is Lieutenant Colonel James Cloud of the Coordinated National Response Team. What is the status of your party?" asked the colonel.

"Well, as you were just informed, we are four strong, we are also mobile and well-armed," Sean answered.

"We are tracking you by your signal; we show you on Route A76 headed south towards Baghlan. Does that sound correct?" Sean looked over at Hasan who nodded his head 'yes'.

"That's the ballpark. We are on the road south headed toward Bagram or maybe Kabul," Sean answered.

"You need to stop and turn around now. The Puli Khumri region is overrun; the valleys have funneled the infected into the two cities and they are being contained by the rivers," the colonel said. "Thermal images show parts of the mass as close as three miles from your current location. If you stay static in your present position, you will see them in approximately twenty-five to forty minutes. They are moving like a swarm of locusts and taking everything in their path."

"No, that's not right. We haven't seen that since the outbreak; they aren't in groups any bigger than ten or twelve now," Brad snapped.

"That's typically correct. When the spaces open, we have seen them disperse into smaller groups, but when confined within geographical boundaries or cities, they are still massing, and they are extremely dangerous. You need to turn around now," the colonel ordered.

"What is your suggestion, sir?" Sean asked.

"You need to put distance on the mass immediately. When you get to thirty point seven miles from your current location, drive due west. You should find a small trail. Follow it up the mountain. The satellite shows the trail, but I cannot verify its condition."

"Then what?" Sean asked.

"Get to high ground, dig in, and hide. This will be your best defense. The mass tends to take the path of least resistance. Wait for the mass to pass you. I will contact you again in four hours. Good luck."

"Wait, we have questions, and we have other survivors on the road two hours north of us." Sean said.

"I'm sorry, Chief. You are not the only group we are tracking presently. I will contact you again in four hours, please hasten your retreat," the colonel said, then disconnected the line.

"Screw that guy Sean! Let's haul ass back to the cave, we can wait this thing out there," Brad said.

"This road empties into a green valley south of here, and there are two very large population centers. The man's story does make sense," Hasan said.

"Well for now we're going to do what the guy said; he is the only connection we have with the outside world. If we sever that tie, we have nothing. Brooks, turn this thing around and step on it. Reset the trip meter, we go west at thirty point seven," Sean said

"On it, Chief," Brooks answered.

13.

Brooks turned the vehicle around and they raced back down the road. Brad kept looking behind them to see the dust cloud of the mass but it didn't come. Within thirty minutes Brooks called out that they had hit the mark. He dropped the Defender into four wheel drive and cut off the road into the rough terrain. The going was now very slow; the terrain was extremely uneven and jagged rocks would often scrape the sides of the vehicle. Sean and Brad had to get out of the truck and guide the Defender across the broken ground.

"We are going too slow. If the colonel was right, we should see signs of the mob any time now," Brad said.

"I know, just keep pushing … Wait, there's the trail, looks like a real piece of shit too," Sean said, pointing. The trail was nothing more than a two-track cut in the terrain; it looked barely wide enough for a donkey. They tried to maneuver the Defender onto the broken path but only somewhat succeeded. Brooks did the best he could maneuvering it up the side of the mountain until the rock walls just got too narrow and he couldn't squeeze it through.

"End of the line, guys. Get out and grab as much gear as you can carry; ammo and water have priority. We move in five minutes," Sean barked. The team grabbed at the gear and started throwing on their heavy packs and attaching rifles. Brad filled all of his pockets with boxes of ammo for his weapons. Anything they couldn't carry they secured in the vehicle. Brooks locked all of the doors and put the keys in his pocket.

"Here they come," said Hasan, pointing at the large dust cloud forming on the horizon. Then they heard the moaning. Sean lifted his rifle to his eye and saw two runners still at least three hundred meters out and closing fast. There were another dozen or so behind them running to catch up.

"Oh look, it seems they sent some of their faster friends ahead to greet us," Sean said, settling into a good prone firing position. "I suggest you boys get moving up that trail now. Let me cut down this advance party and I'll be right with you."

He put the cross hairs on the lead runner's chest and pulled the trigger. The heavy 7.62 round hit the primal's center mass and knocked it off its feet, severing its spine. Quickly, Sean adjusted his aim to the next crazy in the pack; squeezing the trigger a second time he hit it low, shattering its pelvic bone. The primal went twisting into the dirt. The rest of the pack was still out of a reasonable range for his rifle so he got back to his feet and jogged up the trail. Finding a place where the cavern walls narrowed, he dropped his pack and pulled a claymore mine from a front pocket. Sean carefully placed the mine pointed back toward the charging primals, then connected it to an improvised trip wire.

When Sean caught up to the group they had just found a place in the mountain that looked climbable. Brooks dropped his pack and pulled out several hundred feet of rope. He tied one end around his waist and the other end to his pack, and then connected his pack to Brad's. Sean did the same with a rope from his bag and tethered his bag to Hasan's. They made loops in the lines which they attached together with D-rings. They clipped the rings to the men and Brooks quickly ascended the rock face, with Sean close behind him.

Brad and Hasan struggled to keep up with the SEALs and soon were falling far behind. When Brad was only a quarter way up the rock face, Brooks pulled himself over the top. Brooks grabbed the rope and started pulling up Brad and the two packs below him. The tension on the rope assisted Brad and his pace quickened. He looked to the left and saw that Sean had also reached the top and was pulling Hasan up just as quickly.

A loud thunder clap shook the canyon and they saw a blast of smoke and dust shoot up the trail from the claymore. Sean yelled to the men to keep climbing, that the primals were less than a hundred meters away now. Brad pulled on the rope and willed himself up the wall.

When their packs were nearly twelve feet off the ground the first of the primals found them. Brad heard them moan and scream, and Brooks yelled at him to keep climbing and not look down. Brad struggled the last twenty feet completely exhausted until Brooks was able to reach down a hand and pull him over the rock face. Brad lay back just as Hasan plopped to the ground next to him in a heavy sweat. The crowd of primals below them was growing louder, and Brad peered over the ledge. There were only about six of them down there now, many with obvious wounds from the claymore, but they were screaming at the top of their lungs.

"Let's shut these fuckers up, Brooks," Sean said, lifting his rifle.

"On it, Chief," Brooks answered.

With three quick shots each, the primals at the face of the wall were silenced. The team began to hear the sounds of the larger mass approaching the trail. It was a thunderous roar, reminding Brad of the sound of a freight train. The dust cloud slowly crept up the narrow trail and blinded them from seeing the floor below.

Brooks turned, put his pack on, and started heading higher up the mountain. The rest got the hint and followed him to higher ground. Soon they were on a very high ledge overlooking the valley that Route A76 cut through. All that could be seen of it now was a cloud of dust. The mass seemed to fill the valley floor like flooding waters filling every crevice within reach. They could hear them rumbling down the trail below. The moaning had stopped with the loss of their prey, or at least they couldn't hear it over the stampede of the mass.

Sean stepped near a stone wall with a high rock overhang and dropped his pack, then took a seat next to it. "Hasan, are you familiar with this place?"

"I am sorry, friend, but I have never been up this mountain. I know a place farther to the west, possibly down the trail below, but it would be more than two days' walk," Hasan answered.

"Fair enough. Well, let's settle in here. I'm fairly certain these things can't scale cliffs, so let's wait for direction from the colonel," Sean said.

14.

They arranged the gear in front of them and took stock of what they had. They evenly divided the ammo, food, and water between the four of them. They built a campsite under the rock overhang but elected not to build a fire; no sense in risking detection with so many primals below them. They leaned back against their packs. Not wanting to waste water on the chemical heaters, they silently ate cold MREs while waiting for the phone call.

Four hours came and went with no word from the colonel. It was approaching evening and the temperature was dropping. Sean took the phone from his pack and checked it to verify he had a good signal and that the battery was charged. Brad looked out over the valley with his binos, and saw that the cloud had diminished. Most of the mass had passed, but they could easily still make out several groups of a hundred or more moving through the valley.

Just as Brad was sitting the binos down, the phone buzzed. Sean reached for it and pushed the speaker button.

"Hello, this is Chief Rogers," he said.

"Good, good, I take it that by answering the phone you are still alive. I can triangulate your phone's location and you seem to be in a fairly decent spot. Unfortunately, the satellite window has closed and I cannot provide you with real-time imagery data until tomorrow morning," Colonel Cloud said.

"Okay Colonel, let's cut the bullshit, what's the plan?" Sean barked.

"First things first, Chief. What is your status?"

"We are four strong, ammo is green, food and water is green," Sean said.

"How much water, Chief?" asked Cloud.

"We have three days; five, if we ration it," answered Sean.

"Very good. By our estimates, the main body of the mass should have passed you. You will see remnants of the mass over the next ten to twelve hours. There is a high probability that large percentages of the mass will linger in the area for weeks; not everything about these things can be plotted to certainty," Cloud said. "You should stay in your current location for at least another ten hours."

"No problem there," Sean said.

"Colonel, this is Staff Sergeant Brad Thompson, can you answer some questions for us?" asked Brad.

"Sergeant, I'm sure you have a lot of questions, but I only have limited time available to you; you're not the only assets I am working right now. I need you and your team to get some rest. Tomorrow I want you to scout to your vehicle, verify it is operational, and wait for my call," Cloud responded.

"Hold on, not so fast, Colonel. I appreciate you helping us out today, but if you don't answer some of our questions, I'm going to end this call and we can go back to surviving. We have done pretty well so far on our own," Sean said.

"Okay, I understand your concerns; go quickly, what do you want to know?" Cloud asked.

"First, there are other survivors, Colonel, close to a dozen soldiers and two hundred civilians are held up at the customs compound in Hairatan. Can you help them?" Brad asked.

"Son, we are aware of the people at the customs compound. At the moment, we do not have resources to assist them, but we are always looking for a way," Cloud answered.

"Colonel, this is Petty Officer Brooks. What's the situation in the States?" Brooks questioned.

"Short answer? We are in a fight for our lives. We were given some prior warning about the attacks and we took it more seriously than most of our allies. After the first strikes, all civilian air travel was stopped and borders were closed. That helped. We still had a few people fall into the coma phase on the longer international flights before we could turn them back. Most of those stories didn't end well. Mexico and Canada both fell quickly. We are not sure why. We did well in the first few days of the outbreak. The fences along the southern borders and the Rio Grande River did a lot to slow the migration. Also the southern border was well monitored and defended; we were able to rally troops from Fort Bliss and Fort Hood to slow most of them. Eventually, there were too many and we had to pull back into hardened areas. Most of the population is living behind walls in safe areas now," the colonel said.

"And what are those?" Brad asked.

"Hmm ... well, currently the Midwest is considered a fortress. Michigan is naturally fortified by the Great Lakes, and we have moved many of our resources there. We are confronting the hordes on the passes in the Appalachians. Everything west of the Mississippi, between the river and the Rockies, is holding well. New York and most of the East Coast fell, as did every other state with a high population and stringent gun laws. Most military installations are well defended and we are pushing back as the primal virus extends in duration. We are in a fight for survival, guys, but all is not lost," Cloud explained.

The U.S. team members looked silently at each other, their expressions bleak.

"I'm sorry, gentlemen, but we really are out of time. I will contact you again in twelve hours. Good luck," the colonel said as he ended the phone call.

"Shit, I don't know about you guys, but I still feel like I'm in the dark here," said Sean.

"So the plan is to just sit here until morning and wait for another call? This trip isn't going so well, is it," Brad replied.

15.

They slept lightly that night. It was the first time they had slept in the open since they'd left the safety of the compound. Even though they were well above the primals, they felt very little security in their perch high on the ledge. Brad nodded off several times, but bad dreams made it difficult to stay asleep so he soon gave up and sat staring at the moon in the distance. He heard a grumble from Brooks and watched him sit straight up, gripping his rifle, sharply looking in every direction before lying back down and instantly drifting back to sleep.

"Night terrors," Sean said, "one of the many benefits of this job."

Brad turned, and seeing that Sean was also awake, said "What happened in Teremez, Chief? How did you lose your team?"

"Not really a highlight in my career, Brad, it's not something I enjoy thinking about."

"Brooks has never spoken about it either; not since the night we first met."

"Getting out of Teremez wasn't easy; we both left a lot back there. Did you know Brooks was getting out of the Navy? Teremez would have been his last mission. Funny how things work out," Sean said.

"No shit! No, Brooks didn't tell me that. I figured he was a lifer just like you," Brad said.

"Ha. Nope, Brooks is a scholar. Don't get me wrong, he is the best at what he does, but he had plans to leave the Navy and go back to school. Guess that won't be happening now."

"What about you, Chief? What will you do when you grow up?"

"I don't know, man, at one time I thought I'd get me some land and a cabin out in Wyoming ... raise dogs. You know, something simple, maybe find me a wife. I've never been good with women, but who knows?"

"Well Chief, I think your plans for hiding out in a cabin in the middle of nowhere are still possible in this brave new world," Brad said, laughing.

"Yeah maybe you're right," Sean smiled. "Try and get some sleep, Brad, going to be a long day tomorrow," he said, rolling back into his pack and pulling his watch cap over his eyes.

Brad was wide awake as he watched the sun come up. He opened his pack and grabbed a protein bar for breakfast. He had very few of them left, but felt today he would need it.

"We have just under an hour before the next phone call," Sean said.

"What's the plan, Chief?" Brooks asked.

"I've been scanning the trail. I haven't seen any sign of them up here, looks like the valley is mostly cleared too. Let's make our way back to the rock face and see if we can get a better look," Sean said as he hoisted his heavy pack to his shoulders. The rest of them strapped on their battle rattle and heavy packs as they joined him for the trek back down the mountain.

When they reached the rock they had scaled the day before, they cautiously looked over and saw nothing. Slowly, they lowered their bags over the side. Sean quickly rigged a rappelling seat and helped Brooks over the edge and down the face of the rock. When Brooks signaled it was clear, Sean told Brad he was next. Then he helped Hasan down. Finally, by setting the rope over a large boulder, Sean was able to lower himself over the wall and recover the rope behind him.

Back on the ground they packed and stowed their climbing gear. The team sat silently, listening to ensure they were alone. The trail was very quiet; there were no signs of primals other than the battered tracks in the sand. When they were confident in their security, Sean gave the order to move out. Brooks as usual took point, and they cautiously made their way back to the Defender. Brooks paused them on the trail several times to listen, but they failed to see or hear anything. When they found the vehicle, it had been shifted hard and was sitting pressed against the rock face at an odd angle.

"Looks like the mass pushed the truck pretty hard," Brooks said.

The team moved to the vehicle and, working together, were able to get it back on all four wheels.

"Check the engine," Sean said to Brooks. Brooks got in the vehicle and it cranked hard, with poor results, but once the fuel had settled back to its normal spots the engine finally turned over and purred back to life. Sean slid his finger across his throat, giving the signal for Brooks to shut off the engine.

"So what do you think, Brooks?" Sean asked.

"Hmm … I think we'll have to back out of here for a ways, but we should be able to turn around where the trail opens up. If you guys ground guide me we can get back to 76," Brooks answered.

"Sounds good. OK guys, let's get hidden in these rocks until we get the call. Brooks, take Hasan to that ledge; I'll be with Brad over there," Sean said, pointing to a large overlook near them. The men split into two parties, moved to their hide positions, and sat silently waiting for the call. Right at the twelve hour mark the phone buzzed. Sean lifted the phone and hit the speaker button.

"Chief speaking," Sean said.

"Good to hear from you, Chief. What is your status?" Cloud asked.

"Four souls; beans, bullets, and hydro are green; transportation has been secured," Sean rattled off.

"Very well, Chief. Imagery satellite is up; if you move quickly you should be able to get through the mountain pass moving south with only light resistance. We are tracking half a dozen masses near the city at the mouth of the valley. We suggest you stick to the west side of the river when the road forks. The larger masses are all congregated to the east. I need you to understand the eastern side is completely overrun, and there are more of them flooding in from up the valley on that side. The Air Force destroyed the bridge across the river in the first days of the withdrawal. So the most dangerous masses will be trapped on the far side of the river, but there will still be resistance on the western side. From the satellite images, most of the primal populations converged on you yesterday, but be on alert as some may have stayed. You will see primals today, Chief, there is no avoiding it."

"Where are you leading us, Colonel? Why don't we just find another route? No disrespect, sir, but this sounds like a great deal of bullshit," Sean said.

"HQ wants to get you through the mountain range as quickly as possible. Travel will be more difficult in the range, but for the time being the primals tend to walk downhill and do not seem interested in moving into the higher elevations. I know you have more questions, but we need you to get moving, Chief. We will talk again in four hours," Cloud said, disconnecting the call.

"I'm really starting to not like this guy," Brad said.

The men moved back to the vehicle and, being cautious, were able to reverse it out of the trail and back into open ground. The sides of the Defender were now heavily dented from its night with the primals, but for the most part it seemed to be holding up well. Hasan boarded the truck with Brooks, while Sean and Brad walked ahead, guiding it over the rough terrain and back to the road.

When they pulled the truck back onto A76, Sean and Brad boarded the Defender. Brooks picked up speed as he raced down the road to the south.

"If we make good time, we can be in the heart of the mountains in three hours," Hasan said.

"Then that is the plan," Sean replied.

It didn't take long before they saw the first pack of primals. It was only a group of about fifteen, but they were immediately alerted to the presence of the team. They all suddenly stopped in their tracks, made a quick change of direction, and sprinted for the Defender. Brooks intentionally steered the vehicle into them, trying to lure them away from the paved surface of the road. When they were within a hundred feet he cut the wheel hard, raced around them, and back to the highway. They had to do this several times before they got to the higher mountain pass.

"This pass continues for fifty kilometers before it opens in the river valley," Hasan said.

The road had narrowed to no more than twenty-five feet wide with high cliffs on both sides. Brooks drove as quickly and safely as possible. He saw primals just as he passed a curve in the road; they stood blocking the narrow canyon. The primals paused momentarily before they moaned and started their charge. Instead of driving through the primals and destroying the Defender, Brooks cut the wheel hard so the vehicle sat across the road with the passenger side windows facing the mob. Quickly Sean and Brad took aim with their rifles pointed out of the windows.

Brooks and Hasan exited the truck. Brooks aimed across the hood, while Hasan climbed on the roof and took up a prone position. They started firing together, and the mob quickly fell apart and separated. Hasan's loud AK echoed off the canyon walls and could easily be heard above the roar of the primals. Brad put the red dot on his targets' necks and pulled the trigger, watching them fall. He didn't know how many there were; he just focused on finding the target, squeezing the trigger, and locating the next target.

Brad was counting the trigger pulls in his head. *Nineteen, twenty, twenty-one*—he knew it would be time to reload soon. But before his bolt locked to the rear on an empty chamber, he ran out of targets. He opened his door and stepped out into the road. The strong cordite scent of expended rounds hung over the primals' stench. He could see a hundred-foot path of dead bodies, and had started to walk forward to examine one when he heard Brooks yell.

"We have another wave approaching! Reload and make ready." Brad dropped his near-empty magazine and loaded a fresh one before leaping back in the vehicle. He looked up, put the dot on the face of the lead runner, and waited for it to get into range. The primal fell to Sean's rifle before Brad could pull the trigger. He pivoted to the right, finding another runner. *One, two,* he said to himself as he pulled the trigger and watched the primal drop. *Three, four, five.* And another fell.

This group was larger, and they had gotten to within fifty feet of the Defender when Brooks threw a grenade as hard as he could into the mob.

"Frag out," Brooks yelled.

Brad watched Sean pause in his shooting to duck his head just before the grenade exploded, then he rose back up to continue working his rifle on the mob. The frag grenade hadn't killed many of them, but it did manage to knock several of them off their feet and tripped up several more. Knocking them down was just the leverage the team needed to gain an edge and finish them off.

This time when the firing stopped, they rapidly loaded back into the truck and sped down the road around the primals' corpses. They didn't see any more in the pass as they made their way onto the road leading to the river valley. When they reached the end of the pass, Brooks pulled the vehicle to the shoulder and Sean stepped out with his binoculars to scout the valley.

The terrain ahead of them was very green and miles wide. They could see the river and how it flowed through the center of the city. Sean traced the river south with his binoculars through the valley and spotted the fork in the road. Just as the colonel had said, several large masses were on the eastern side, trapped there by destroyed bridges. Scanning further, there appeared to be one main road along the western bank of the river. For the moment the approach looked clear, with only small packs of stragglers in the streets. Sean walked back to the Defender and approached the team.

"Okay guys, we're going to roll through town weapons hot. I can see bad things on both sides of the river, but the eastern bank looks the worst. With the condition of the road, we can get through this valley in about ten minutes," he said.

"Cloud said to stay away from the eastern side?" Brooks asked.

"That's correct, we're going to hit this fork in the road and stay on the approach running along the west bank until we get out of the city. Brooks, you drive hard, man; no stopping. If we have to hit them, slow down to under thirty so you don't crush the fenders," Sean said. "Keep your windows down and armor and gloves on. I don't want glass getting broken. Remember, controlled shots. Priority targets are those in front or to the sides, we can outrun the rest. Do you have any questions?" he finished.

"What if they mob the road? Are we going to shoot at them?" Hasan asked.

"If the road is blocked, then Brooks will hit a side street until he is free to break south again. I'm hoping the weapons fire will draw the crazies to where we *have* been, instead of where we are going. I realize it's a risk, but those things will be moaning anyhow, so going silent won't help us," Sean said. "If there are no more questions, top off all of your magazines and let's mount up."

Brad didn't say a word during the brief. He didn't have a good feeling about this op. It was clear that the colonel wanted them to move through the city, and the intel did appear to be solid. Brad just didn't get the urgency. Why it was so important for them to get through the valley today? Why couldn't they wait until things cooled off more? He moved back to his spot in the rear passenger side of the Defender, topped off his M4 magazines, and pulled the spares he kept in his rucksack.

He sat in the back seat and positioned all of his extra magazines in the pocket attached to the seat in front of him; after that he made sure the twelve magazines in his vest were secure. Brad checked the slide on his M9 to verify a round was chambered; then he pulled the Sigma pistol from his pack and eased it into a strap on his protective vest. Lastly, Brad removed the suppressor from his M4 and placed it in his day bag before putting in his ear plugs. He had a feeling things were going to get noisy.

Brad looked to his left and saw that Hasan had made many of the same preparations. Hasan looked nervous, which made Brad smile. Brad was sure he looked just as bad; he looked at his outstretched, gloved hand and could see it shaking. Brooks took notice of what Brad was doing and grinned at him.

"Hey don't worry about the shakes, bro, that's just your body getting loaded full of adrenaline," Brooks said. "Worry when they *don't* shake before a fight anymore."

Brooks pulled the Defender to the center of the road looking down into the city. He paused there for a moment and looked at Sean.

"Is everyone ready for this?" Sean asked.

Brad gave a reluctant thumbs up, and Brooks revved the engine. Sean gave Brooks a nod, and the Defender leapt forward and down the hill toward the city.

They were making good speed when the first of the primals came into view: a skinny man dressed all in white. It was standing just on the corner of the road as if it was waiting for a bus. When the primal saw the speeding vehicle, it put back its head and let out the moan. At first nothing happened, but after a few long seconds, Brad watched in horror as all down the street primals ran from doorways and out of hidden alleys.

"Remember gentlemen, head shots will kill them, but any hit that fucks them up counts. Just keep them off of our vehicle," Sean shouted over the roar of the engine.

They were beginning to form a mob, but were not very well organized. Instead of running into the street to block the vehicle's path, they ran directly at the Defender. This was an advantage to the team. Because of the speed at which Brooks was driving, they were able to get past many of them. Brad watched several run from a side street and he raised his rifle. It was next to impossible to get good shots through his optics, so he reverted to his iron sights and attempted to put lead on the target.

He fired as fast as he could, watching rounds hit them in the chest and sides. Some were knocked down but others kept running. He dropped his empty mag and loaded a fresh one. He saw a group of them just clearing a wall. They were moving fast and on an angle that would meet with the Defender. Brad focused on the lead runner and fired two quick shots. He watched the runner's neck snap to the side as it veered off the path, tumbling and rolling into others. Brad took sight of another and put on heavy fire, missing several times. He saw the thing stretch out its arms to grab him. Brad flinched back in his seat as the primal flew by and crashed into the rear side of the vehicle.

Brooks drove on. Keeping a straight track, his speed was approaching fifty miles an hour but he didn't take it above that; Brad knew he didn't want to hit a primal at terminal speed and destroy the vehicle. Sean had dropped his heavy rifle, had his MP5 shouldered, and was laying controlled shots into the faces of the advancing crazies. Meticulously, he pulled the trigger and they went down, tripping up others behind them.

Now they were pouring from the streets like bees from a hive.

"We have a problem," Brooks shouted over the barrage. Brad looked up and saw the street ahead was beginning to fill up with the things.

"Cut right at the next street. We can find a way around," Sean ordered.

"Hold on!" Brooks yelled as he hit the brakes and turned the wheel hard to point the Defender down a side street. He hit the gas and plowed through two primals that were able to get in front of the vehicle. Brad was rocked forward into his seat and turned to the side just as one of them crashed into his side of the Defender. He saw the arm of the primal reach past his face, grabbing at anything within reach. Brad pulled back his rifle and pointed at the sternum of the creature. He shoved the rifle forward, listened to the hot barrel sizzle on its naked chest, and fired twice at point blank, knocking the primal back.

Three more fell in front of the vehicle as Brooks cut the wheel hard to the left and into a southbound street. Brad looked left past Hasan and saw the passing alleys were filled with the creatures that were now changing direction to get back at the team. Brooks drove fast, outrunning several of them. More than once he had to brake hard just as he hit one and launched it out of the way. Brad's M4 barrel was cherry red from the speed with which he had been firing, and he was down to the last spare magazines that he'd put in the seat pocket.

"There! That's the road that leads out of the valley," Sean pointed. Brooks put the pedal down and aimed for the side street. As he made the turn, he hit the brake hard and slammed the Defender into reverse. Brad bounced off the seat in front of him and quickly determined the reason for Brook's hasty maneuver. The street was filled with them. Brad looked behind and saw that they were quickly becoming surrounded.

Brooks raced the vehicle in reverse up a side street and cut down another to try to stay ahead of the mob.

"Hold on everyone, this is going to get ugly," he said as he pulled the emergency brake and cut the vehicle hard, spinning them in the opposite direction. Brooks pressed the accelerator all the way to the floor. The Defender roared again and picked up speed as it crashed through waves of primals.

"We're not going to make it out," Sean yelled. "Brooks! Look for a place to hold up."

Brad tried to pretend he hadn't heard the exchange and concentrated on firing out of the jumping, rolling vehicle. He knew his fire wasn't very effective so he slowed his breathing and tried to aim before taking every shot.

"Duck!" Brooks screamed just as he cut the wheel hard to the right and crashed the Defender through the front of an open shop. The vehicle exploded through the block-and-glass storefront, coming to a rest against a lunch counter with the ass end of the vehicle sticking through the wall.

The room was filled with smoke and dust. Brooks and Sean were already out, putting lethal fire on the mob trying to squeeze past the sides of the vehicle. Brad tried to open his door but it was pinched shut. He couldn't reach the buckle of his seat belt, so he pulled his karambit and cut himself free, then dove through the window. Brad hit the floor hard, head first, and he tried to right his body. The firing was loud and Brad could barely hear Sean and Brooks calling out targets to each other.

Brad, back on his feet, reached through the vehicle, grabbed Hasan's arm and dragged him across the seat. Hasan realized what he was doing, turned and rolled through the open window. Brad looked around the room and saw an open stairway leading to the roof. He pointed Hasan in its direction, then went to the base of the stairs and fired over the top of the Defender and into the crowd. Hasan ran past him and called from the top that the roof was clear.

Sean looked back, nodded, and as he pulled the pins on two grenades, yelled, "Fall back to the roof, frags out!" He tossed the grenades and Brad saw Brooks throw two more. Both men peeled away from the entrance and charged up the stairs to the roof, pushing Brad in front of them.

They reached the top just as the four grenades exploded in rapid succession. The blast threw a cloud of dust across the street in front of the store. Brad looked over to see Brooks slapping a small, shaped demo charge at the top of the stairs. "Fire in the hole!" Brooks yelled.

Brad lifted himself up and ran for the far corner of the roof. Just as he reached it and ducked his head, the loud *THUMP!* and concussion rolled him over and into the wall that lined the roof.

He must have been knocked unconscious because he found himself laying on his back looking into the sky. His ears were muffled through the ear plugs, but he could still hear the frenzied moans and screaming of the primals. He rolled to his belly, lifted himself to a knee and looked around. There was a large hole in the roof where the stairs had been. Brad resisted the urge to look over the wall, knowing he would find the screaming mass below him. He dropped to his ass and leaned against the wall. Hasan was farther down, sitting in the same position with his rifle across his lap. Sean and Brooks were standing and looking into the hole.

"Good, you're awake. Are you hurt?" Sean called out to him.

"Fuck if I know, I can't feel shit right now," Brad yelled back at him.

"That's called shock, bro, embrace it, 'cause when it wears off you're really going to feel like shit," Brooks said.

"What's going on?" Brad asked.

"Well, current situation is F.U.B.A.R. (fucked up beyond all recognition). The demo charge on the stairs has stopped them. Unless they learn to fly or make a fifteen-foot primal pyramid, I think we're safe for the time being. But we ain't getting off the roof," Sean said.

"I'm going to choke the shit out of the colonel, if I ever meet him, for sending us through the city," Brad said.

16.

The battered team sat and listened to the primals below. The creatures' strategy hadn't changed; they would just pound against the walls of the building and moan. They paced below like dogs that had treed a scared animal, looking up and howling in frustration at the men they knew were on the roof. The team avoided looking over the edge; if the primals saw them they would become frenzied and more would be drawn in. When they did risk a peek, they found the tops of hundreds of heads pressed against the rear of the Defender, waiting for a turn to squeeze into the broken storefront.

The hole in the roof was nearly fifteen feet to the floor, and the stairs had been blown clean away. Nothing would be walking up them today. Structurally, the roof was hurting from all of the abuse thrown at it. It creaked and groaned when they walked, but it was still standing and that was all that mattered. The outside walls were made of stone and block, and they were high, too high for the primals to climb and too strong for them to push down. They were secure in their hide as long as the building stood.

Brad reached in his pack, pulled a bottle of water and took a small sip. He didn't have a lot and didn't know how long this would have to last him. He didn't even want to think about food, knowing all of it was in the vehicle below. He looked at his watch; it was approaching time for the colonel's call. Brad was pissed at the man and was certain he'd intentionally led them into the dangers of the city. With all of his technology he had to have known the city would be infested.

The phone buzzed. Sean reached over and pressed the speaker button before sitting it on the roof. The men adjusted their positions to gather around it.

"Good afternoon gentlemen. From the satellite images and the location of your phone, I can tell that your travels have not gone well," Cloud said.

"No disrespect, Colonel, but go fuck yourself!" Sean shouted at the phone.

"Excuse me Chief, but before we get into formalities, could you please give me your status?" Cloud replied.

"Roger that SIR! We are four souls, ammo black, food black, water red, transportation fucked," Sean said sarcastically.

"I see, and thermals show you are pretty well surrounded. We must have underestimated their numbers. Could you verify that, Chief?"

"Oh yes SIR! We are positively surrounded. Thank you for the help with that by the way."

"Okay Chief, I need you to calm down and listen. In approximately two hours we will have air assets on station. They will be delivering a large number of two-thousand pound bombs to the city in front of you," said Cloud. "These drops will be danger close and you will need to take cover as best you can."

"What the hell! You're going to blow the shit out of us, Colonel!" Brad exclaimed.

"This is our best and only option. The lab folks tell me the blast and shockwave should kill, or at least temporarily immobilize, any primals in your immediate area," Cloud said. "As soon as possible after the last bomb detonates, you will need to beat feet, by vehicle is best. Either way, you need to be gone before the primals rebound. Do you understand?"

"Hold up, Colonel, thanks for the help and all, but are you telling me you're pulling air assets away from the States just for us?" Sean said.

"Don't flatter yourself, Chief. Unfortunately, we have a high value individual in country that requires your talents, and you are the only ground assets within a thousand miles. We are assisting you, so that you may later assist us. Be prepared for the bomb strike, gentlemen, next contact will be in twelve hours," Cloud said, disconnecting the call.

"What the fuck was that?" Brooks said.

"Assist them? This guy is tasking us! Doesn't he realize we're all messed up and stranded on a roof?" Brad said. "I really hate that guy."

"Okay fellas, let's calm down for a minute. All good shit, but let's worry about that stuff when we're far gone from here," Sean said.

Brad stood and walked to the edge of the roof. It was a little more than a thousand yards from the building to the river, and maybe a mile to the road that left the valley. "Where are they going to squeeze two-thousand pound bombs into here? This entire place is danger close!" he said, looking at the surroundings.

They were stuck on a strip of the city about three miles long by half a mile wide. It was tucked in between the mountains and the river, the majority of which was on the far side of the river.

"I don't know, Brad, but two or three of them would be enough to incinerate this place. I think we need to start making plans for our egress," Sean answered.

"I shut off the Defender when I left it, so the engine was running after the impact with the building. No guarantees it will start though, and I don't know if I can back it out," Brooks added.

"From this location, it is less than four kilometers to the pass. If we make it to the opening, we can head into the mountains. There is a mountain trail that bypasses the highway. I think it best to stay off the roads now," Hasan said.

"I'm with Hasan, traveling by vehicle is turning out not to be much fun. I know it's slower but maybe we would be better in the mountains. Even the colonel said they don't like traveling uphill," Brad said.

"Okay, let's wait till the drop before we finalize plans; we have options and that's enough for now. We need to fortify something and build a bunker with whatever we've got. We'll take cover in the back corner of the roof, face down. As soon as the bomb run ends, be prepared to drop in and clear the building. If we can make use of the Defender we will. If not, we will have sixty seconds to grab bags and haul ass," Sean said. "Break down, clean, and inventory your gear. I want an accurate count of what you got and what you need from the Defender. If Cloud is on time, we can expect drops in the next sixty minutes."

Brad leaned back against the wall and slowly started placing his gear on the roof in front of him. He still had all of his M4 and M9 magazines minus the ones he'd had in the seat pocket. The Sigma was still stuffed tightly into his body armor. He was carrying no food, and his camel back was almost dry. It would be a long night if he had to move out on what he was carrying. Brad compared notes and the rest of the team was in similar circumstances. They made a list of necessities they would pull from the Defender in case it was immobile. The list was broken down by location. Brad and Hasan would take the grunt work of pulling and carrying gear from the vehicle. Sean and Brooks would be on security and trying to make the Defender roadworthy.

Brad looked over and saw that Brooks had finished his inventory and was starting to pile the broken pieces of concrete into a shelter against the far corner of the roof wall. Hasan had gotten to his feet and was helping Brooks construct the makeshift bunker.

Brooks, peering through the hole, said it was a clean drop to the floor and he could see the primals in the store were anxious to get at them on the roof. Brad could hear them fighting with each other as rival packs joined together in the cramped space of the store—screaming and clawing, the ripping of clothing and the snapping of jaws—humanity had really been brought to the level of ravenous animals. It had been over forty minutes since the phone call with the colonel, and the primals were still frenzied below them, not giving up easily on their trapped prey.

Brad finally spoke up. "Sean, what do you think of this high value person the colonel talked about?"

"Your guess is as good as mine, but they must be pretty desperate to put us on the mission," Sean answered. "We are pretty well trashed as it is here. For now, I say we take Cloud's help, then when we are clear of this mess we will look at our options."

Brooks was sitting in the corner cleaning his weapon; he looked up and nodded his approval. "I really would like to know who we are dealing with. I have never heard of this Colonel Cloud, and we work in a very small community."

"I know what you're saying, Brooks, I've had some of the same concerns about him. But for now, all we got is him and his bombs so let's keep rolling with it," Sean said.

He was intently studying his map and comparing it to what he saw on the ground in front of him. Brad watched Sean stuff everything in his pack and look at his watch. "Okay boys, less than ten mikes; let's dig in and wait for the rain," Sean said.

The men sat huddled in the hastily-made bunker and waited. It had begun to grow quiet as they lay motionless and out of sight of the primals. The sun was still high in the sky and the temperatures still sat close to a hundred degrees. Brad cautiously peeked out over the walls and saw the swarms of primals moving about in tightly packed clusters. Occasionally two groups would merge, but for the most part they stayed independent and fought with each other when the fringes of a group would meet. Brad wondered if the groups had dominant leaders; they would be interesting to study if they weren't always trying to kill him.

His thoughts were interrupted by the sudden buzzing of the phone. "Chief here," Sean answered as he put the phone on speaker.

"Roger Chief, this is Thunder Turkey, flight commander for today's mud mission. This is your brief—you will be getting three total passes: one to mark and draw targets; two with lethal drops. We know where you are based on briefed imagery. Please mark your location with an IR strobe if available. These drops will be danger close. We will try and keep you out of the blast zone and the drops as close to the river as possible, but you know how these things work. Keep your heads down; it's going to get loud for you. These are two thousand pounders. I recommend you keep your mouth open, breathe shallow, and cover your ears. Gentlemen, do you have any questions?" the voice asked.

"Uhh ... I guess not. Just don't kill us. Strobes are lit," Sean answered.

"Very well then. Good luck gentlemen, you have four birds less than ten minutes out. I recommend you get moving right after the second lethal drop. From experience, these bombings stun the primals but not for very long. Thunder Turkey out," said the voice as the call ended.

"Well you heard the man, let's tighten up," Sean said.

Brad was pressed against the back wall of the makeshift bunker watching the sky when he saw the first jet screaming in slow and low; it looked like it was floating in the clouds. "Guess there's no reason for them to make high fast drops on these guys, not like they can shoot back," he said.

They heard the thunder and watched the jet fly a tight line along the team's side of the riverbank as it started launching flares and metallic decoys that burned a bright white and made a whistling sound as they flew.

"Never seen those before," Brad said.

"Me either, but looks like they seem to be doing the whole 'mark and draw' trick the pilot talked about," Brooks replied.

Brad watched as the primals lost focus on the store; they started walking at first, then running toward the noise near the river's bank. The jet finished its run and peeled away, banking high into the sky. Brad watched as three more jets dropped in slow over the mountain. They were a lot higher but still gave the impression of floating. He watched them line up with the river, then their ordnance began to drop and scream in. Brad tucked his chin and covered his ears; he left nothing but the heels of his boots facing the river.

Brad felt the ground thrust under him as the first bombs hit. The blast wave seemed to levitate him off the surface of the roof. Then the shockwave hit the building with a force that rattled everything and dumped pieces of the makeshift bunker on top of the team's flattened bodies. The low wall that surrounded the building's roof held, and helped to somewhat direct the blast up and away from the men. The thunder was horrific, and the dark mushroom clouds blocked out the sun. Brad heard the debris rain down all around him. This wasn't the first time he had seen a bomb run, but it was the first time he had been this close.

Brad's teeth were still rattling in his mouth when he heard the scream of the jets lining up for their next run. Again he tucked his chin, covered his ears, and tried to make himself one with the surface of the roof as the next round of bombs hit. Again the roof shook underneath him and the blast wave pounded and heaved at the sides of the building, knocking the air out of him. Brad froze himself in place until he heard the debris stop raining down, then he slowly got to his knee. The air was filled with dark black smoke. Brooks and Sean were already up, rigging a rope to the roof, and preparing to drop into the building.

Brad saw that Hasan was still curled in a ball next to him; he reached out and slapped his hip. Hasan slowly rolled to his back and asked him if it was over. Brad nodded and extended a hand to help Hasan to his feet, then they made their way to the hole's edge. Brooks had already dropped in and cleared the room.

Sean handed the rope to Brad, who quickly dropped into the hole and watched Sean and Hasan slide down behind him. Sean immediately made his way to the rear of the Defender and took up a security position. Brooks was behind the wheel and eagerly working to start the vehicle.

Brad made his way to the back door and was trying to wedge the gear out of the cargo space when he heard the Defender roar to life. "Everyone on board!" Sean yelled as he squeezed out through the opening and into the street. Brad stopped what he was doing and crawled through the rear window. Once he was in, he reached back and pulled Hasan in behind him. Hasan was visibly rattled from the bomb drops and just sat forward with his rifle between his legs. Sean slapped the back of the truck and yelled that the street was clear. Brooks stomped on the accelerator and the Defender scraped and crunched backwards out of the store front.

Brooks turned the vehicle hard to the right when he cleared the opening and Sean jumped into the seat next to him. Brooks again gunned the vehicle and it roared as it crunched over the broken glass and debris that filled the street. Brad looked out of the cracked windshield between Sean and Brooks. The streets were filled with rubble and the bloodied bodies of the primals. He was horrified to see some of them in broken and twisted positions still trying to lift themselves to take chase. The closer they got to the river, the worse damage they found. The road was barely passable where the concrete surface had heaved and buckled.

"We're not going to get far in this," Brooks said. "The engine temp is climbing and I have a Christmas tree of warning lights on the dash."

"Well, ride her hard as far as it will go," Sean answered.

"I always do," Brooks retorted.

He dropped the Defender into four wheel drive and carefully eased the vehicle through the broken and twisted concrete.

"Eyes up back there fellas, I don't know how long the shock will keep them down," Sean said.

Brad looked out his window; this close to the river, there wasn't much of anything resembling a human. All he could see was crushed buildings and garbage. Smoke was still thick in the air and fires were burning everywhere. *This city of primals has been given back to the earth*, he thought. Brooks drove as fast as he dared and soon they had cleared the blast area and the streets started to open up. The flares and decoys must have done their job drawing the primals into the danger zones, because there were still none of them in sight.

Brooks eased the Defender onto the hard-packed highway. He cautiously dropped back into two wheel drive and accelerated. They made it a good two miles into the valley before they started to hear the engine squeal.

"I'm sure she's cooking. I think we punctured the oil pan, and the radiator is trashed. We're running damn hot," Brooks said.

"Understood. Try to find Hasan's trailhead or at least a break in these mountains before you stop," Sean replied.

Brooks continued to nurse the vehicle down the road; it was still screeching and had started to leave a trail of blue smoke. He found a deep cut in the rocks that led to a trail, and pulled the Defender over and ahead to the entrance. Brad watched Brooks reach down and turn the key, shutting off the Defender for the last time.

"Okay boys, dismount and 360 security. Let's get eyes on this location right quick," Sean barked.

Brad tossed his small pack out of the window and crawled out after it. He took up a hasty security position just to the rear of the vehicle. He looked around and saw that the rest of the men had equally spread out and were searching their sectors.

"Looks clear here, Chief," Brad said, and heard simultaneous replies of the same from the rest of the team.

"Okay, break down this vehicle. We need to be moving into these rocks ASAP!" Sean hollered back and he turned to move towards the vehicle.

"How well do you know this area, Hasan?" Brad asked.

"I have traveled this road often, and I have had the misfortune of seeking shelter in these hills before to evade your patrols," Hasan answered.

"Good! Then you take point," Sean said, smiling at Hasan.

It took them several minutes to break down the Defender. Brad felt the weight of his overstuffed pack when he heaved it to his shoulders. They had evenly distributed all of the food, ammo, and water between their packs. Brad was beginning to feel like a pack mule with the crushing weight of his load. He walked to the rear of the Defender and leaned his pack against the rock wall to try and take some of the weight off of his shoulders. He watched as Sean made a quick pass around the vehicle to make sure everything usable had been removed. Brooks took the keys from his pocket and laid them on the seat of the truck. Then Sean pointed to Hasan and signaled for him to lead the way.

Hasan went forward with his AK47 cradled in his arms. He moved up the large crack in the rocks to a narrow trail that led steeply up and away from the road. Brooks walked directly behind Hasan, and Sean took up the rear. Brad struggled to walk the steep incline and almost fell several times.

"Do not lose heart, friends, the path will become easier at the top," Hasan called back to them. They climbed for several minutes longer, carefully stepping over loose boulders. At the top, as Hasan had said, the path dropped over the face of the rock, then flattened and slowly snaked up the mountain on the other side.

"I want to get as much distance on this place as possible before nightfall," Sean said.

"What about the colonel?" Brad asked.

"Don't worry about the colonel right now. Our job is survival, and that means getting as far as possible from that valley," Sean answered. "Let's try and make that ridge before we look for a campsite, Hasan," he said, pointing to a high piece of terrain far in the distance.

Hasan nodded, stepped off on the trail, and set a quick pace. Moving fast, Brad felt the burning in his shoulders where the weight of the pack's straps cut into him. His feet were swollen and he could feel every stone on the path through his faded and battered boots. *It's going to be a long day,* he thought to himself as he concentrated on just putting one foot in front of the other.

The trail wound in and out of the face of the mountain. The surface was well worn and dusty, made up of mostly packed gravel and stone. As the elevation increased, the air thinned but it was still just as hot. The trail was quiet and they took several breaks where they would take a knee and listen. So far nothing was following them and the colonel's advice that the primals avoided traveling uphill seemed to be true. Even though they were exhausted, they made good time and pushed each other down the trail. After several hours, they had finally arrived at the approach to the ridge.

Hasan stopped on the trail and sat on his rear, leaning back against his pack. He pulled a bottle of water from his pocket and took a long drink. "I wanted to warn you, when we pass the top of this ridge you will see the way is packed with hundreds more ridges just like this one. The trail appears to go on forever, but do not be disappointed, friends, it is less than two days' journey back to the next pass and to the highway. We will see a village on the way," he added. The men nodded as they lay back on their packs and drank from their own supplies of water.

After several minutes, Brooks got to his feet and extended a hand to Hasan, pulling him from the ground. They turned and made their way up the path to the top of the ridge. At the top they found the path widened and twisted into a large rock overhang. Under the overhang they could see remnants of an old campfire, evidence that this place had been occupied before. In the distance, the path wound at a slow downslope away from the ridge before it cut out of sight. As Hasan had said, the ridges stacked up and seemed to go on forever. *The next couple days are going to suck,* Brad thought.

They made camp in the overhang. The men dropped all of their gear and Hasan went off to gather wood for a cooking fire. Sean made his way to the overhang and sat down heavily.

"We will stand watch tonight in two-hour shifts. Let's stay in this hide until long after daylight." Sean pulled the phone from his pack and turned on the power before resting it on a rock. "We'll have to be careful with the batteries now that we don't have the Defender to charge them," he said, then pulled two cans of slop from his pack and tossed them near the fire pit. "Here guys, let me buy you dinner," he said before he leaned back against his pack.

Hasan returned with the wood and built a small fire. Brooks stacked rocks around it to conceal the flames from anyone or thing that might be nearby. Then he pulled the cooking pot from his pack and started the evening meal. They sat without talking and watched the fire, mainly due to exhaustion, not from a loss of words. Brad had little appetite but knew he had to eat if he were to have the energy for tomorrow's hike. He took his portion of the slop and settled back against his pack and ate in silence.

Just as he was finishing he heard the phone buzz. Sean let out an exaggerated sigh and pressed the speaker button.

"Go for Chief," he said.

"Good evening, Chief, I trust your egress from the city went well. Could I get a status report?" Cloud said.

"We are four strong. We are packing heavy ammo and rations; probably enough water for two, maybe three days," Sean said.

"Well gentlemen, the satellite shows that the river's bank was nearly leveled by the bombing runs. What primals there are seem to be dead, or dying, based on thermals," Cloud said.

"Would have been nice if you could have cleared the city before we went through," Sean barked.

"Once again Chief, we have limited air assets and even less fuel. We are running off the strategic oil reserves right now and we have to be very careful with what we've got. Your breaching of the city was a risk we had to take; fortunately things worked out well," Cloud answered.

"Screw you sir! We almost died out there and now we are on foot and who knows where the hell we are at," Sean barked again.

"Let's calm down. I can see from the last satellite pass that you have drifted from the road that we recommended you stick to. I'm going to need to you make course corrections back in that direction," Cloud said.

"Not going to happen Colonel! We are going to stick to these mountains until we hit the next pass. Our guide on the ground is leading this exhibition and he has been more reliable than you at the moment," Sean said, nodding to Hasan, who nodded back in recognition.

"Chief, you do understand that you and your men are still members of the armed forces and obligated to follow orders?" Cloud asked.

"Understood, Colonel, please send out the MPs to make my arrest; I'm ready to go to the brig," Sean responded sarcastically.

"Very well, Chief, have it your way. If you stick to the mountain path you will find some very rough terrain. The trail will break near the village of Shurazar," Cloud said.

Sean looked to Hasan, who nodded, indicating the colonel was correct.

"What intel can you give me on the village, Colonel?" Sean asked.

"The village is very small, not many details in the record. We don't know the state of infection, but it is somewhat isolated off the main road so you may get lucky. We will run satellite recon on the site during the next window," Cloud said.

"And what is your plan for us beyond this march?" Sean asked.

"We will talk when you reach Shurazar, Chief," said Cloud, disconnecting the call.

"Wow, he sounded pissed," laughed Brooks.

"Yes, but we have the leverage right now. He needs us for something, that's the only reason we have him. Probably the same reason they waited so long to call," Sean said. "Let's get some sleep, we have a long walk ahead of us tomorrow." He rose to his feet and grabbed his rifle to take the first watch.

It was dark now and the temperatures had dropped this high in the mountains. Brad leaned back against his pack and watched the fire; it was burning low but the coals still put out considerable warmth. The men knew it wasn't a good idea to have a fire out in the open at night, and was completely unheard of in military operations, but they were going by new rules now. Brad pulled his feet close to him and undid his boot laces. He immediately felt relief as he pulled the worn leather from his feet. A hot shower would be nice, but they barely had water to drink, they couldn't waste any for bathing. Sinking deeper into his pack, he rested and watched the flames lick at the rocks they had placed to conceal the light of the fire.

He didn't know how long he had stared at the flames; he couldn't see past the glow of the fire. He looked to his left and saw Hasan sleeping soundly. Brooks was next to him, out cold with his rifle in his lap. Startled, he saw Sean standing across from the fire, looking out at the mountains.

"What is it Sean?" Brad asked. He got no answer to the question; Sean just stood there silently. Brad looked harder to see what Sean was doing, but he couldn't make out his face in the shadows. Brad got to his feet and walked around the fire.

Sean was still standing in the same spot looking out into the mountains, his face darkened by the shadows.

"Sean, what is it? Do you see something?" Brad asked again. This time the man turned and Brad found himself looking into the face of PFC Ryan. His face was contorted in a scream and his eyes were nothing more than shriveled black holes. Ryan grabbed at Brad's jacket and pulled him close to his face, then pulled his head back and let loose the primal moan. Brad screamed and dropped to his back, digging his feet into the ground to try and escape. Ryan fell on top of him and began shaking his arms while making the primal moan into Brad's face.

Brad woke to Brooks shaking him awake. He was covered in sweat and his feet were scraped where he had pushed himself back into his pack and against the rock ledge. Brad looked across the fire and saw Sean looking back at him.

"You okay buddy?" Sean asked.

"I'm fine, just another bad dream," Brad said. He looked over at Hasan who was also awake now. Hasan gave him a knowing nod and rolled over and went back to sleep.

"I'll take the watch now if you don't mind Sean, I won't be sleeping anymore tonight," said Brad.

17.

They woke early the next morning and prepared their packs for the day's march. They opted for a cold breakfast since none of them were in the mood to build another fire. Brad volunteered the cans from his pack, happy to lighten his load. The sun was just peeking over the mountain and the valley was covered in an orange glow. The temperatures were still cool and Brad was wearing a heavy fleece he always carried with him.

"We should reach the village by late day," Hasan said.

"What are we going to find there, Hasan?" Brad asked.

"I have been through this village several times. It is very small, only a few families there, shouldn't be many more than a hundred," Hasan answered.

"Taliban, Al Qaeda?" Brooks asked.

"Is there such a thing anymore? It is only us and them now," Hasan laughed. "No friends, these were always peaceful people. They are quiet and keep to themselves; we will have no problems from them. Unless of course they have turned."

They finished their conversation and hoisted the heavy packs to their backs. Hasan once again led the way, with Brooks close behind him and Sean in the rear. They walked more slowly today, comfortable that they were not being pursued by the primals. The team skirted a high ridge line that had several cutbacks lowering them deeper into the valley. It would have been a beautiful sight under different circumstances. The sun was all the way above the mountain now, and the light warmed Brad's face. He frowned, knowing that the sun's same warmth would later torture him with its heat.

Sean and Brad walked side-by-side, feeling more relaxed in the deep isolation of the trail. It was impossible to keep up the high mission tempo for days on end, and it would kill them if they tried. Back on base they would go run their missions fueled by adrenaline, but they would always have the safety of the base to return to. Here in this new war they rarely found down time; they were always on edge with no home to return to. They were feeling the burnout, the complacency that could kill a soldier on the front lines.

They put their trust in Hasan; they were in his playground. The man was a machine. He had grown up fighting wars. He had his rifle slung across his back and he kept a slow but steady pace. He would pause when going around a blind corner, and would halt the small patrol if he felt uneasy and need a closer look. The going was slow but had also been uneventful.

They walked for hours without seeing any evidence of a primal.

"So, Sean, I've heard all of the theories, but what do you make up these things, really? Are you still sticking to your lion idea?" asked Brad.

"I don't know anymore. I thought eventually they would starve or something and die off. You remember all those movies with the zombies? These things don't act like that; they don't stagger around asking for brains, and they don't rot," Sean said. "They hunt, you've seen them. They gather in packs and sniff the air like hyenas."

"It's de-evolution, bro," added Brooks. "I mean, we evolved from animals, and this shit is just taking us back. The virus backed us up a good ten thousand years of progress, back to the caves, brother."

"They are demons. We are being punished for our actions," Hasan said. "These days will not end until we learn to work together and stop fighting each other."

"And if that never happens?" asked Brad.

"Then we all die," Hasan answered.

They walked without speaking after that until Hasan called a halt at the top of a hill that overlooked the trail ahead of them. They all took a knee and sipped at their emptying bottles of water. "Past that bend is the village," Hasan said, pointing down the road. There wasn't much to see. The terrain was identical to what they had been following the entire day: a long dusty trail skirted by high walls on both sides. The trail suddenly went to the right at the bottom of the hill. They would be approaching blind.

"Brooks, you proceed with Hasan, Brad and I will shadow you off the trail to support your move," Sean ordered.

"Sounds good, Chief … Let's go meet your friends," Brooks answered as he slapped Hasan on the back and started walking out down the hill.

Sean helped Brad to his feet and they made for the far rock wall. They cut the corner so that they could observe their two men on the road and still see the approaches to the village. They were in the shadows now, nearly invisible to Brooks and Hasan. Sean moved quickly so that they were parallel to the trail, but still out of sight. When they reached the turn in the path, they waited for Brooks and Hasan to clear the wall before, one at a time, they ran the corner to the far wall and again ducked into the shadows.

They could see the edges of the village now; there was no movement. Sean found a large ledge about eight feet off the ground that overlooked the approach. He used Brad to hoist him up, then reached down and pulled Brad up behind him. Lying flat on the ledge, Sean readied his large scoped rifle and observed the village. Brad took the cue from Sean and pulled his binos from his pack and started scanning the village for targets.

Brad watched Hasan walk the trail. When he had gotten to within feet of the first home he stopped and raised his hands. Brad could hear Hasan's words echo off the walls of the canyon, but couldn't make out what he was saying. Brad saw Brooks standing beside Hasan in a protective but relaxed posture. His rifle was slung and his arms were crossed. Brad continued to scan but saw no movement.

"You got anything, Sean?" Brad whispered.

"Nothing, my scope is clear," Sean said.

They watched Hasan walk beyond the first house and stop in the street. Brooks followed and again took up a position beside him. From his high location Brad could see the entire village. It wasn't much. It probably didn't qualify as a village at all; this was a very remote place. It was more of a ranch or community farm by American standards. Brad counted maybe five homes and just as many out-buildings. If it was a farm, it was suspiciously absent of livestock and crops.

Hasan continued to call out as he walked further into the square that the houses lined up on. He received no answer. He looked back and spoke to Brooks. After a moment, Brooks turned to face them, put his hands in the air, and waved them forward. Brad helped Sean drop to the surface below before he dropped over the edge himself.

They met in the square. There were three small homes on the south side of the trail and two larger ones on the north side.

"The elder lived there," Hasan said, pointing to one of the large homes. "I have been a guest in that home; I have slept on the roof in the cool night air."

"Well, let's clear that one first then," Sean said as he walked toward the home's front door.

They approached the house and stacked up along the far wall. Brooks was directly in front of the door, waiting to kick it in on Sean's signal. They all had their rifles at the ready, and Sean held up five fingers and began to drop them one at a time. Before he could drop the last finger, the door handle moved and the door clicked open.

Brooks took a quick step back and readied his rifle. The door opened a good ten inches but it was dark inside, and they couldn't see past the shadows. Brooks yelled in his best Dari for whoever was inside to come out. They stopped and listened but heard nothing. Brooks readied a grenade. Hasan raised his hand, stepped in front of Brooks, and quickly entered the house. Sean looked at Brad, shrugged his shoulders, and they followed Hasan inside.

With the door fully open the light filled the room. It was bare, just a dirt floor with a large rug laid in the center and no other furnishings. There was a small fireplace and just to the left of it was a long hallway that led to the back of the home. Brad went inside and took a position in the corner aiming down the long hallway. Sean and Brooks followed suit in opposite corners. Hasan, with his rifle low, walked down the hallway calling out in Dari. When he reached the end of the hall, they heard a child's voice.

Sean lowered his rifle and down the hallway toward Hasan. Brad could hear the two men whispering.

"Room is clear, come on back, guys," Sean called out.

Brad looked over at Brooks who just shrugged at him; Brad turned and walked down the long hallway. At the end, he found a darkened room with beds and chairs along all of the walls. It was filled with women and children and an old man in a corner. Brad counted at least twelve women and just as many children. Hasan was kneeling in front of the old man, holding his hand and whispering in his ear.

Hasan looked back at Sean and Brad before speaking. "This is the elder, his name is Sayed," he said. "He says this is all that remains of their village. They live only in this house now, the others are empty," Hasan finished.

"Where are the men?" Sean asked. Hasan translated the questions and Sayed spoke slowly in a hushed voice.

"He says his village stopped receiving visitors one month ago, so his men gathered the stock and took them to market but they never returned," Hasan said.

The old man continued speaking. "He says they waited three nights, and then the rest of the men gathered and left to search for the missing, and they also never returned. Now it is only them. He thinks the Americans may have taken them. He says he has seen no soldiers or fighters in weeks, we are his first visitors," Hasan said.

The old man stretched out his arms with his palms up and the women began to weep. Hasan grabbed the old man's hand and softly spoke to him until he put his hands back in his lap. "He said he is ready for you to take him away, he wants to join his sons now," Hasan said.

Sean stepped into the hallway and motioned for Brad and Brooks to follow him. "Well this is a real mess," he said.

"They think we took their men away. Who wants to be the one to tell them we are the good guys and it was the boogey man that took them all away?" asked Brooks.

"Or better yet, that they are more than likely all dead or turned," Brad added.

Hasan stepped into the hallway and leaned against the wall. He now had his rifle slung over his shoulder. He dug through his pack and took a long drink from his water.

"The elder remembers me. He believes me when I tell him we are not here to take him away. I told him we did not take his people," Hasan said. "They have no idea what is going on outside of this canyon."

"Hasan, I'm sorry but I am going to leave that work to you. These are your people, I'm sure you will think of something. Can you ask if it's OK if we hold up in one of the houses here? And where is the water?" Sean asked.

"I already did. The elder says we may use the house next door, it was his oldest son's home. The water flows from a spring located behind these homes. Go ahead and prepare yourselves, I will stay with these people for a bit longer." Hasan frowned and put the cap back on his bottle and walked back into the room.

Brad followed Sean down the hallway and out into the street. They slowly cleared the large house next door and investigated its spaces. They found the house to be identical to the elder's. There was a large entry room with a rug on the floor and a hallway leading to two smaller parlors. The stairs led to a large room on the second floor filled with beds. There was an entrance to a balcony that had a ladder leading to the roof. Brad climbed up it and looked out over the small village. He heard a noise and looked to find Sean following him up the ladder.

"Should we clear the other building?" Brad asked.

"Normally I would, but I think we'll be OK. There's the spring," Sean said, pointing. "Let's get some water together and start boiling. It's probably clean here in the mountains but why take the risk?"

18.

Brad lay on a bed in the corner of the second story, his gear on the floor next to him. He was feeling the frustration of their trip and was second guessing himself about coming. They had strayed from their original mission to try and get to the airbase and hitch a ride home, and they weren't finding anything out here but death and misery. Maybe he should have stayed at the compound. He glanced around. Brooks was on a rack across the room methodically cleaning his weapons. Sean was in a bed in the other corner sleeping.

"What do you think of the colonel? Do you think he has a plan to get us home?" Brad asked Brooks.

"I don't know, man, I'm sure to those folks we are completely expendable. I've conditioned myself not to rely on the brass anymore," Brooks answered.

They heard the buzzing of the phone. Sean lifted his head and swung his feet into a sitting position. He reached down and answered the phone, placing it on speaker.

"Good evening, Colonel," Sean said.

"I see you have reached the village," Cloud said. "Can you give me your status, Chief?"

"We're good. What's the word, Colonel?" Sean snapped back.

"Well gentlemen, your bypass away from the road and the loss of your vehicle has delayed us quite a bit. Anyhow, your team has been selected for an operation," Cloud said.

"You have got to be fucking kidding me?! Colonel, I don't have a team, and we are far from operational!" Sean yelled at the phone.

"Chief, you just said yourself that you were good! And I know that conditions are not ideal, but you are the only ground assets we have in country," Cloud snapped back.

"What's the op?" Brooks asked, shrugging his shoulders at Sean.

"Classic snatch and grab," Cloud replied.

"Are you fucking kidding me, and who is the target?" Brooks questioned.

"His name is Aziz, originally from Syria. He was a low level man before the outbreak, but now we have reason to believe he was involved in the planning of these attacks. Aziz may also possess advanced information on the origins of the virus. We also believe he was involved in the weaponization of the virus."

"Whiskey Tango Foxtrot!" Brad said.

"That is correct, Sergeant. We need Aziz. The Centers for Disease Control believe he may be the key to cracking the virus," Cloud said.

"Come on Colonel, you know I would need a six-man team at *least* to attempt a snatch. I have two operators, a grunt, and a local militiaman. You really think we are the best for this job? Can't you just drop another team in?" Sean argued.

"I'm going to be honest with you guys; the remaining joint chiefs don't believe this mission is worth the assets. Months ago they would have given us a team, but now? The CDC has worked hundreds of leads and we are running out of resources. You are all we've got."

"Now hold up, the joint chiefs? Who *are* you, Colonel? Who are you working for?" Sean asked.

"Chief, I already explained my position to you—I am with the Coordinated National Response Team," Cloud said.

"Which means?" Sean snapped back.

"In earlier days, I would have been considered a military liaison to the Central Intelligence Agency," Cloud answered.

Brooks stood up and walked closer to the phone sitting on Sean's bed. "So you are just another spook hanging us out to dry. Does SOCOM even know we are alive?" Brooks asked.

"Gentlemen, we have strayed off topic. Your status has been reported up, and you are under my operational control. I need you to prepare to copy the mission parameters. I can assure you that if this mission wasn't of the upmost importance we would not be speaking. If you ever want to make it home you better start following instructions," Cloud said.

Sean reached into his cargo pocket and removed a pad of paper. "Ready to copy when you are, SIR!" he said.

19.

Brad found himself sitting on the roof with the rest of the team. They were huddled around a map of a small cave complex to the west of them. Hasan said he was familiar with the area but had never personally visited that cave. The colonel had said that Aziz was in a small group, hiding only with his wife and two of his bodyguards. From the colonel's rainbow-and-puppy-dog description, he should be easy to take down.

If they successfully captured Aziz, the colonel had promised them transport home. That was Brad's only motivation for this mission. He didn't believe that one man in a cave would be the solution to all of this, but if that was the ticket home, he would give it his best.

Sean had thoroughly inspected their gear. He advised the men that they were not equipped for the mission but would have to make do. The hard part would be in taking Aziz alive. They also didn't know what the man looked like and he would be with at least two other armed men who would most likely want to kill them. It would be good times all around. Sean ended the brief and suggested the men clean up and get some rest.

Brad laid his pack and bedroll out on the bed on the second floor; he saw the bundle of letters from his men. He picked them up and felt the weight of the stack before stuffing them back in his pack. He wished he knew how the group was doing at the compound. He wished there was a way to contact them to let them know what was going on. He made a mental note to again ask the colonel more about them.

He visited the stream. Stripping out of his uniform, he stepped into the water and was finally able to clean the days of dirt and grime from his bruised and tired body. He knew he wasn't supposed to drink the local water, but after being chased by monsters and eating shit from cans, he barely cared anymore. He dropped his head deep into the cold water and took a long, refreshing drink. He lowered his full body into the clear water and lay against the bank, finally relaxing for the first time in days.

He heard a noise behind him and quickly stretched across the bank for his Sigma pistol sitting atop his small pack.

"It is okay friend. It is only me, Hasan," Hasan said, walking from the shadows.

"Shit Hasan, I thought you were a primal, buddy," Brad said.

"It is okay, I will not disturb you for long. Take these clothes, the women have volunteered to wash our clothing. They will have it back for us in the morning," Hasan said.

"Oh, okay," Brad replied as he saw a woman pick up his clothing from the bank and replace them with a white shirt and pajama pants. Brad blushed at the sight of the woman and sunk deeper into the water.

"Damn, Hasan! You could have told me she was there," Brad said.

"Sorry friend, I was not aware that you were afraid of women. They will have our clothing cleaned and ready for us in the morning. Brooks already retrieved your other uniforms from your pack. You and the others can rest tonight; I will stand watch with the villagers. Good night Brad," Hasan said, walking away.

Brad climbed out of the cool water and stood on the bank, letting himself air dry before putting on the clean cotton shirt and pants. The light material felt good against his skin and was a welcome treat from the dusty uniform. He slowly made his way into the house and through the empty room.

He walked up the stairs and found bowls of rice, vegetables, and dried lamb sitting on a table. Sean was wearing a similar pair of white pajamas and was already digging into the food. "The elder said as welcome guests we were entitled to a good meal," he said.

"What happened to that guy?" Brad said, pointing at Brooks snoring away on his rack, also dressed in the pajamas.

"Looks like a full belly and clean clothes knocked him out," Sean said laughing.

The next morning they found, as the women had promised, all of their clothing had been cleaned and folded. Brad found his uniforms in a neat stack at the foot of his bed when he woke up. He sat himself up and also found the food bowls from last night had been replenished with bowls of dates and nuts. There was also a tray of foot bread and a pot of tea. Brad was starting to feel guilty that these people were giving up their valued food stores for them, but he also knew it was the way in their culture and it would be rude to not accept the gesture.

He found Sean and Brooks already stuffing their faces. "Try the tea, it's not bad," said Brooks.

Brad ate while he dressed. He was overjoyed with the clean uniforms, especially the socks. He repacked his bags and loaded all of his items in the appropriate places. It would be a half-day's walk to the hiding place of the man they called Aziz, and another two hours to climb up to the cave complex where he was known to be hiding. The colonel said that satellite photos had confirmed that Aziz was still there, so it would be up to them to grab him.

When Brad finished dressing, he carried his gear down to the large entry room where Brooks and Sean were waiting. "Have you seen Hasan?" Brad asked.

"No, not all morning, he slept in the main house last night," Brooks answered.

They carried their gear outside and into the street. They were dressed in full battle rattle ready for the day's march. Hasan was outside waiting for them. They went over the plan and Hasan drew them a large map in the sand. He described to them how to reach the base of the mountain, and where the most likely approaches to the cave would be found.

"Hold up Hasan, are you not going?" Brooks asked.

"No my friends, I cannot," Hasan said.

"What do you mean you can't? We need you Hasan," said Brad.

"Look around you, Brad, these people need me. The elder asked me to stay, to help him protect his family. I fear my family is lost after seeing the dead city in the valley. I will stay and help to protect these people, they are my mission now," Hasan said.

"I cannot argue with that Hasan, and I don't blame you," Sean said, reaching out to shake the man's hand. "If we ever have the means, I will contact the compound and give them your location. Maybe one day they will have the ability to come for you. We won't forget about you, Hasan."

"And I wish you all good luck in your travels … Now go before you lose the light," Hasan said, obviously trying not to choke up on his words.

The men exchanged hugs and handshakes before lifting their heavy packs to their backs and turning to face the road. They solemnly started their journey without the assistance of their Afghan guide. Brad turned around to look at the small group of homes one more time before they faded from his view. He saw Hasan standing in the middle of the square and he waved to him one last time before turning to walk away. Brad knew Hasan had made the correct decision, but he was still sad at losing a valued friend.

20.

It was late in the afternoon when they reached the highway again. The mountain trail, as Hasan promised, had taken them around the dangerous primal-populated valley. The men sat in the shade eating a light lunch as they consulted their map. It was another two miles to the trailhead that led to the mountains, then at least a mile's climb to make it to the mountain trail that would bring them to the cave. They wanted to reach the caves just before dark. They still had night vision and that would give them the edge over Aziz.

The team moved along the last two miles of the road in a staggered column. Brooks was in the front taking point and Sean was on rear security. Brad walked in the middle of the column on the opposite side of the road. Now that they were back on a mission, they felt themselves become more tactical again, and with the presence of the caves, who knew if there would be enemy nearby. The colonel had misled them before and they didn't want to take any chances.

Brooks put his fist in the air and signaled a halt. They had reached the beginnings of the trail that would lead them to the mountains. It wound up steeply away from the road and cut into the side of the rocky terrain. They still couldn't see the caves, but they tightened their formation and slowly moved up the path. The trail was very rugged and cut steeply up in several locations. Eventually it leveled out high in a plateau-shaped formation near the base of the mountain.

They took a knee while Sean scanned the rock face and stone slopes ahead with his binoculars. "I can see the trail leading to the cave, and I believe I can see the mouth of the entrance," he said. "Let's hide our heavy gear here. This is a good open spot for a helicopter landing or whatever the colonel sends to extract us."

"I was thinking about that. If the colonel could send a helicopter to get Aziz out, then why didn't he use that to bring a capture team in?" Brad asked.

"Maybe they have more helicopters than SEALs," Brooks said. "You know what, bro? We're already committed, so let's just keep our heads on mission okay?" he said, smiling over at Brad.

They hid their heavy rucksacks in a crevice in the rocks and covered the opening with brush. All they carried now were their light day packs filled with ammunition and water, and all of their weapons. Brad missed his armored plates for his vest. It had been a while since he had faced a human foe. He didn't know what scared him more—a terrorist behind a gun or the primals.

"Let's go silent and stay concealed," Sean said as he indicated for Brooks to move out.

Brooks again led the way on point, with Brad close behind them. They moved with stealth now, pausing often to just watch for movement and listen for the faintest of sounds.

The going was slow; even though the distance was short, it took them another two hours to get within view of the cave's entrance. They pulled up into a hide in a broken rock formation just as the sun was beginning to set. Brad estimated they had less than an hour of daylight left. He looked through his binoculars, scanning the cave entrance while Sean looked through the powerful scope on his rifle. Brooks was a few feet away in charge of rear security making sure someone or something didn't sneak up on them.

"There! I have movement," Sean whispered. From the mouth of the cave they saw a man and woman walking together. They passed the entrance to the cave and kneeled in the late sunlight. Two men came out from behind them and took up a position to the left of the cave entrance. Only one of them was carrying a rifle slung across his back and looked very relaxed. The two men looked to be joking with each other, as one stopped to light a cigarette.

"Let's assume the male with the female is Aziz. The other two playing grab ass and catching a smoke are the bodyguards," Sean whispered. "Male wearing red is our target. Bodyguards are in blue. All three are bearded; this should be fun in the dark. OK, let's get comfortable, we have confirmed the cave is occupied. We should be getting a call from the colonel just after dark with the go order."

Brad adjusted his pack in front of him to pad the rocks that had started to cut into his elbows—it wasn't perfect, but it helped. He scanned all along the face of the mountain with his binoculars but saw nothing else of interest. The rock face was jagged and worn, but the trail itself looked well-traveled and shouldn't be very difficult. Brad hated walking on busted trails at night with his night vision; the lack of depth perception always made for a clumsy trip.

As the sun dropped behind the mountain, the cave entrance was quickly consumed by shadows. They had to switch to night vision to see anything. Brad pulled down the optics on his helmet to look at the cave; it was still too far away to get a clear image. Sean had advanced optics on his rifle, and it was now his responsibility to watch the entrance.

Right on time the phone buzzed. This time Sean answered with an ear piece to observe noise discipline. "Go for Chief … we are only three, Hasan opted out … we are locked and cocked … yes, we have verified that the cave is occupied. We had a visual on four individuals: one female and three males. I believe I have confirmation of Aziz … Roger that, we will obtain the package and return to flat ground … Roger, we will signal the aircraft with IR strobe … Roger we have sixty minutes … Hooyah, Chief out." Sean finished the call and stowed the phone back in his pack.

"Okay let's move. Brooks, you have point. Brad, you have the rear security now. Keep it tight," Sean whispered.

They moved quickly and quietly up the trail. There was a full moon in the sky and the night vision was functioning perfectly. The trail was well-traveled and they could see that it had even been improved with stone steps.

When they approached the cave entrance, Brooks raised his fist and they took a knee. He tossed up hand signals indicating he was going to scout the entrance and he moved ahead. Brad watched him walk slowly and hunch low near the entrance of the cave. He stepped just inside the mouth and turned on the IR headlight attached to his goggles. He sat and listened patiently before waving the rest of the team forward. Sean and Brad fell in just behind Brooks, then they slowly made their way inside.

They found themselves in a long tunnel. The ceiling was just high enough that they could stand straight up, even though they were already walking at a crouch. There were benches at the base of the tunnel walls and old and battered ammo crates, probably long empty. They moved cautiously down the corridor until they reached a corner. They saw a dim light coming from around the bend. Brooks again called a halt as he grabbed his goggles and tipped them up and away from his eyes.

Brad watch Brooks slowly move his way to the edge of the corner and peek around it. He pulled his head back and let his silenced MP5 relax on its sling as he drew his fighting knife. He looked back at Sean. Sean nodded and Brooks rounded the corner. There were no sounds of struggle, but within minutes Brooks came back into view dragging one of the guards behind him.

Brad moved past the downed bodyguard and fell back in line with the two SEALs. They stacked up on a battered plank door. There was a light coming from inside so they removed their night vision optics. Sean peeked inside between the boards and confirmed that the other three targets were there. Brooks removed a small charge from his pack and placed it on the door. He looked at Sean and Brad and held up ten fingers, then dropped to nine. They moved away from the door and looked away, covering their ears.

With a thunder clap and a bright flash the door exploded in. Sean and Brooks charged in after the blast before the smoke had cleared. Brad was momentarily stunned but quickly got his bearings and followed them into the dimly lit room. Brooks had already taken down and was flex cuffing the second bodyguard. Sean had Aziz in a headlock. Brad scanned the room and saw the female on her feet running for the bodyguard's rifle. He dove across the room and caught her in a flying tackle that crushed her into the floor. He lifted himself off her while maintaining pressure and put a knee in her back while he flex cuffed her hands behind her.

In under a minute it was over. They had Aziz cuffed, blindfolded, gagged, and lying face down on one of the beds. The female and remaining bodyguard sat against the wall with their hands behind their backs. The female was screaming hysterically and there was no calming her down, so Sean put a strip of duct tape across her lips when she refused to be quiet. Brooks lifted Aziz into a fireman's carry and started heading out the door.

"Don't leave us," the man pleaded in perfect English. Brad stopped and turned back to look at the man. Then he looked at Sean, who shook his head

"It's your call, Brad, but they can't come with us," Sean said as he followed Brooks out of the room.

Brad saw a large knife on a table; he took the knife and threw it on the ground a few feet in front of the man. "Wait until morning, then cut yourselves free. If you follow us, I will kill you," Brad said as he turned to walk away.

Remembering Hasan's words about demons, he stopped and turned again. "There are other survivors who can help you, but you have to join our fight against the primals," he said.

"Yes ... of course ... anything," the man said with tears in his eyes.

"Take the woman; there is a village: Shurazar," Brad said.

"Yes please, I know this place," the man begged.

"They have a militia there; go to them in peace and they will help you," Brad said, walking away. "Do not leave this room until morning or we *will* kill you."

Brad hurried out the door and down the hallway. When the light faded, he put his night vision back on. He caught up with Sean and Brooks near the cave's entrance. Sean led the way to make sure it was clear, then stepped off at a quick pace. Brooks followed him, carrying Aziz. They followed the path back to where they had left their bags. Going downhill now and at a near jog, the return trip didn't take long. Brooks dropped Aziz heavily by an outcrop of boulders. He checked Aziz's bindings, then left him to prepare his own gear.

Sean told them to turn on their IR strobes—small beacons attached to their gear, which flashed an invisible light that only the extraction team would be able to see through their optics. "It's been forty-five minutes, prepare for the bird's arrival," Sean said.

They stacked and readied their gear, then took a knee facing out to watch the horizon. They heard it first: the thumping of the blades coming in from far away. The Black Hawk flew over them low and without lights before it circled back and landed with the door facing them. A man dressed in a flight suit and carrying a collapsible field stretcher jumped from the door and ran to them.

"Where is Chief Rogers?" he asked.

"I'm here," Sean said.

"Good evening, I'm Mr. Douglas. Do you have the package?" the man asked.

"Right there," Sean said, pointing at the body on the ground.

"Okay then, follow me," Douglas said. Running to Aziz, he dropped the stretcher on the ground and quickly assembled it. Brooks took the hint, dumped Aziz on the stretcher, and assisted in strapping down his arms and legs. Then Brooks put on his pack and grabbed one of the stretcher handles. Brad took one last look behind him in the direction of the cave before he helped Brooks carry the stretcher laden with Aziz to the helicopter.

They jumped on board, placing Aziz and his stretcher in a rack, then Douglas boarded and closed the door behind him. Douglas squeezed past the crew chief's seat and fell into the co-pilot's position. Sean yelled something but no one could hear him over the roar of the now lifting helicopter. The man signaled toward the ceiling, and Sean saw the headset and put it on. Brad and Brooks looked up and did the same.

"Where is your crew chief?" Sean asked over the intercom.

"We are running short of those these days," Douglas said. "We are lucky to even have this bird; it's one of the last ones in country."

"You Army, Mr. Douglas?" Brad asked.

"No, I wish. I'm just a civilian. I fly ... well I guess I flew ... for the oil companies, but I'm on an indefinite government contract now. As long as they feed me and keep me alive, I fly. This here is Captain Bradley. He's retired Air Force," Douglas said, pointing to Bradley.

Bradley raised a hand to wave but said nothing.

"They pulled us out of Bahrain for this mission. Not that there was much worth staying for once the survivors' camp was overrun. The island has pretty much been written off. Just small pockets of resistance held up in skyscrapers mostly. There isn't shit left of the place now," Douglas finished.

A flashing yellow light and the piercing beep of an alarm started to flash from the console. "Get ready to exit, we will be landing soon," he said.

"Landing? Where are we? We haven't been in the air long enough," Brooks asked.

"This flight is only getting us to a refuel point; we don't have fuel for much else. We made it to you fellas on fumes as it is," Douglas answered.

"We will be coming around once to check for screamers, then I'm going to set her down by those rocks near the fuel bladders," Bradley said.

"Understood, Bradley," Douglas answered.

The Black Hawk banked hard and circled out over the open sand, then came back and set down in a cloud of dust. Bradley and Douglas reached around the cockpit and started flipping switches as the helicopter started to wind down.

"Chief? Would you and your boys mind stepping outside and setting up security?" Douglas asked.

Sean reached down and pulled the large bay door open. The three of them stepped into the cool night air. The blades of the helicopter were slowing but still making a good deal of noise. Brad had his night vision back on and was scanning the desert.

"Looks clear, Mr. Douglas," Sean said. "Where are we?"

"We are just south of Kandahar, and we need to hurry. Mr. Aziz's ride will be here soon," Douglas said.

Douglas and Bradley grabbed a large canvas bag from a cargo compartment in the helicopter and ran a distance from the bird. Douglas dumped the contents of the bag onto the ground.

"Chief, could your team handle this? Headquarters said your men would be familiar with this gear," Douglas said. "I would offer to help, but the captain and I really have to get the refueling done before the screamers show up."

Sean ran to the spot and examined the gear. "You gotta be shitting me," he said.

"What is it, Chief?" Brooks asked.

"It's a damn Fulton! We don't use this shit anymore," Sean said.

Douglas looked back over his shoulder and yelled, "We do now, Chief. Could you get it set up please? The pickup will be here in under twenty minutes."

"I'm not following. Sean, is there another helicopter coming?" Brad asked.

"No, the Fulton is a big ass balloon. We're going to strap it to Aziz. An aircraft will fly overhead and catch the balloon, then reel his sorry ass on board. We trained on these but they stopped using this gear years ago," Sean answered.

"Well, nothing is too good for our boy Aziz," Brooks said, gesturing back towards the helicopter. "Let's get it done, Chief."

Set up was fairly straightforward. The kit bag contained a balloon, a gas bottle, a harness and about five hundred feet of heavy line. First, they tightly strapped Aziz into an orange jumpsuit that was connected to a large, heavy-duty harness. Brad stuffed a bundle of letters into the jumpsuit and tightly zipped it shut. Brooks saw him and gave Brad a knowing nod, as he forced Aziz into the harness and tightly strapped him in. Next, they attached the coiled line to the balloon. Finally, the other end of the line was secured to the harness and they waited for the signal from Douglas that it was safe to inflate.

"Has anyone bothered to explain to Aziz what is about to happen?" Brad asked.

"Nah, we figured a surprise would be better," Sean said.

Douglas called out that the aircraft was near the approach and to inflate the balloon. Sean connected the gas bottle to the balloon and turned on three IR strobes connected to a section of the line. Then he turned the valve and the balloon began to quickly fill with helium. As the balloon filled, Aziz figured out what was going on and he began to panic.

"Don't worry pal, you're going to love this," Brooks laughed while slapping a heavy pair of goggles over Aziz's eyes.

The balloon filled quickly and pulled off the ground, trailing the line behind it. There was no breeze, so it went almost straight up and barely drifted. The line was now taut and all the slack was gone. It was very quiet now; all they could hear was the sobbing of Aziz and the fuel pumps purring away, filling the large tanks on the Black Hawk.

Douglas called back to them again from the fuel bladders. "The C130 says they are on approach and they have visual. You might want to step away from our guest."

"C130? So why didn't they just land and pick all of us up?" Brad asked.

"Not so easy, son. All of the airfields near here are overrun; this is the best we got," Douglas answered.

They heard the buzzing of the C130 coming in from the east. The moon was now covered in clouds and they could hardly see anything. Aziz increased his panic when he picked up on the sounds of the approaching aircraft. The men stepped away from Aziz and gathered near the helicopter to resume their security watch of looking for primals.

The aircraft got louder as it got closer and lower to the ground. Soon Sean pointed and they could just barely make it out flying low and slow toward them. A large, V-shaped hook extended from its nose and it was on a direct path for the balloon. The C130 flew directly over them. At first nothing seemed to happen, then they saw the line stretch and Aziz snapped into the air and was gone.

21.

The flight crew was finishing up the refueling procedures. They turned heavy wheels and pulled switches to cut off the power to the large pumps. Brad watched them as they disconnected and stored the heavy fuel lines in plywood lockers. Captain Bradley and Mr. Douglas walked back to the Black Hawk, diligently inspecting every detail.

"We are almost ready to go, Chief. If your boys could continue to pull security until she is warmed up I would appreciate it," Douglas called.

"We got it sir, just tell us when to mount up," Sean called back.

"You're going to need to make it quick, sir, I got movement," Brooks said.

"What do you see Brooks?" Sean called out.

"Large mass at your three o'clock and moving fast."

"The birds bring them in, for some reason the screamers love helicopters," Bradley called over his shoulder.

Brad raised his scope and saw them, a small party out front and another larger group trailing them. Sean snatched up his long rifle and took a prone firing position; Brooks fell to the ground near him with his own scoped rifle.

"You work the center, I'll pick up stragglers," Sean calmly said to Brooks. "Brad, keep an eye on our flanks, I don't want anything sneaking up on us."

Brooks began firing his rifle and methodically knocked down the leaders. Sean followed his lead and started firing in a smooth motion to cut down the runners, but it was doing very little to slow the pack's progress. Brad ran to the edge of the clearing in a high spot where he could see all the approaches to the landing site. He could see the mass closing on them from Sean's direction. Brad continued to scan wider, checked the rest of the area, and found it clear.

The Black Hawk started to wake up; the rotors slowly went into motion, whooping as they sped.

"Chief, I have the mini-gun up if you and your men would like to retreat to the bird," Douglas screamed over the increasing whine of the turbines.

"You heard the man, bound back," Sean ordered.

Brad turned around and ran back to the Black Hawk, Just as he arrived from the flank, he could see Sean and Brooks board the bird. The engines were screaming now as Bradley increased the throttle. Sean took up a position behind the large M134 mini gun, flipped the switches powering it up, and readied himself to fire.

"You're clear to engage, Chief," Douglas called back.

Sean pulled the trigger and a stream of rounds cut through the night; a blinding laser light show ensued. Brad could no longer see the primal mob with his night vision off, but he followed the trail of gunfire and watched the shadows dance as rounds exploded and skipped off of the ground. Sean was decimating the crowded path as he cut left and right, sweeping through the charging primals.

The Black Hawk slowly lifted with its nose down and began to pick up speed. It turned slightly and headed into the mob that was now far below. They reached out their arms and grappled at the beam of gunfire Sean was pouring down on them. The Black Hawk opened the distance and Sean continued to fire even though the threat was now gone. He cut a wide path through the charging mob, releasing weeks of frustration.

"Cease fire, Chief, we may need some rounds for later," Douglas called back.

Sean shook his head and powered the gun down. Leaning back into the crew chief's seat, he looked exhausted. He intentionally set down the headset before he closed his eyes.

The Black Hawk flew smoothly through the night sky speeding south. Brad looked out of the small window but could see nothing but blackness. The desert was dark; there were no lights, no signs of life. He didn't see a single fire, no headlights on the roads. It was desolate and dead below him. He pressed back against the hard seat and tightened the restraint belt.

"Where are we going, Mr. Douglas?" Brad asked.

"South to the Arabian Sea; with all of the tanks full, and if we fly conservatively, we should make it. If not, we will have some walking or possibly swimming to do," Douglas answered.

"Well that's reassuring. We catching a ride on a Navy vessel then? That how we're getting home?" Brad asked.

"Wish I could answer your questions for you, son, and as good as a Navy meal sounds right now, unfortunately that's not where we are headed," Douglas said.

"Enough with the riddles! Where the hell are we going?" Brooks asked impatiently.

"We are scheduled to land on a secured oil platform off the coast; the Navy and Marines have secured a number of them in this area. Land-based facilities are all closed this side of Iran," Bradley said. "I know it's not ideal boys. I'm not excited about it myself. But it sure beats the hell out of nesting with screamers."

"Then what?" Brooks asked.

"Then we wait. We were promised a ride home when we took this job. I don't have the details. I just have to get this crate to the platform," Bradley said. "I have been told it has power, food, and hot showers, so let's just take it one day at a time."

Brad sat back in his seat, shaking his head, his body finally giving in to the exhaustion. *It's going to be a long ride home*, he thought to himself.

Thank You for Reading

If you have, an opportunity please leave a review on amazon.

Lundy W. J. (2013-05-09). Tales of the Forgotten. Kindle Edition.

Whiskey Tango Foxtrot: Volume II

Visit W.J. Lundy on Facebook

Volume I Whiskey Tango Foxtrot. Kindle Edition.

Book three

Only the Dead Live Forever

Now Available.

Made in the USA
San Bernardino, CA
07 May 2014